DEAREST
TRAITOR

BY
PATRICIA WILSON

M I L L S & B O O N L I M I T E D
ETON HOUSE   18-24 PARADISE ROAD
RICHMOND   SURREY   TW9 1SR

*First published in Great Britain 1992
by Mills & Boon Limited*

© Patricia Wilson 1992

*Australian copyright 1992
Philippine copyright 1992
This edition 1992*

ISBN 0 263 77505 4

*Set in Times Roman 10 on 11¼ pt.
01-9204-56891 C*

Made and printed in Great Britain

CHAPTER ONE

GEORGINA reined in at the crest of the hill, her hand stroking over the satin neck of Stardust. Ears like velvet pricked up in response and the little filly made a slight movement of her head. They understood each other, rider and animal especially attuned, a small unit of belonging because this was Georgina's own horse, the chestnut raised from a foal. No one else had ever ridden her, nor would they even think of it. For one vital moment she was content, her eyes sweeping over the well-loved scene. Adversities might come and go, even small, poignant tragedies, but this went on forever, the only real love of her life—Kellerdale.

In front of the horse and rider the land fell away in a green wooded valley and then rose quickly to high, rolling hills, the great sweep of the Dales as far as the eye could see. As far as the eye could see, too, the land belonged to Kellerdale Hall, the great estate of the Templetons since Norman times. Once they had owned more, but even now Georgina knew she could ride all day on Templeton land, never challenged or halted. It was still a small, benign kingdom, and she a favoured subject.

It gave her a great sense of peace, happiness, because she was and always had been an integral part of everything—the land, the family, the magnificent old hall with its gleaming windows, ivy-covered stone, tall chimneys and acres of parkland. To Georgina, part of them and yet not part of them, this was home and she loved it fiercely.

She narrowed her long tilted eyes against the wind, her soft mouth tightening. Everything would stay the same here but only on the surface. *Now* there was trouble, tall blonde trouble, and it was here to stay because she knew for sure that nothing would be able to dislodge Auriel Delafield: Malcolm was going to marry her. A new factor was to be added to perfection, a disturbing element to ruffle the calm days. Already there was uneasiness, polite discord. She wanted to march right in and put things right, but it was not her place. She was merely an outsider who loved them completely.

Georgina and Stardust snorted in unison, mere chance but she patted the filly firmly, quite sure she too had noticed the faint air of distress and disbelief that now hung over the family. Long ago she would have talked it over with Steven—but that was long ago. She didn't think of Steven now. He was banished from her mind, banished for four years and it was permanent.

Celia Templeton rode up the hill and stopped beside Georgina, but neither of them spoke. Celia was blonde too, but it was a cool, regal blonde like Northern sunlight, her eyes the clear Templeton blue. The two girls were a startling contrast to each other, Georgina's eyes the colour of honey, black-lashed and long, her hair dark red, caught in a plait that almost reached her waist. It glinted with changing lights in the cool sunshine, now red, now almost golden, now deepest mahogany.

At the side of Celia's slender height, Georgina looked tiny. She was vivacious, and as alert and racy as the horse she rode. Laughter sat easily on her face and often a mercurial temper, but today her ready temper was under strict control. From now on she would have to be a steadying influence, help whenever possible and keep quiet for the rest of the time. It looked like being a lasting arrangement.

For once Celia was on the boil, and Georgina recognised all the signs. The two girls were lifelong friends in spite of their different social status.

'Isn't she *awful*? Malcolm must be mad! And that name! *Nobody* is called Auriel!'

'Malcolm must love her. He's come home engaged to her,' Georgina murmured, her doe-like eyes scanning the home woods. There was a tree coming down there. She would have to get the men out to it.

'Bah!' Celia snapped. 'Did you hear what I said, Gina?'

'I did.' Georgina kept her voice calm, never looking round. 'You said "Bah!". Nobody says that except in comics. It's probably not even a real word, and, anyway, she's Malcolm's problem.'

'She's *not*! She's a family problem. Mummy's gone all vague. I know the signs and so do you. It's the way Mummy copes when things are horrifying.'

Georgina smiled to herself, her practised eyes still scanning the woods and the nearer fields. She had noticed Lady Evelyn's retreat into haziness, her delicate, aristocratic face faintly pained. Once or twice during the last week her eyes had caught Georgina's and she had looked like someone hanging on to sanity with hopeful determination. Georgina loved them, all of them, but now a viper was in their midst and there was nothing she could do about it.

'Gina! Will you stop working?' Celia turned exasperated eyes on her friend. 'We've got to do something about this before it's too late.'

'It *is* too late,' Georgina pointed out firmly. 'Your brother is engaged to Miss Delafield and, short of paying somebody to kidnap her, there's nothing we can do. And I'm not working. I'm all ears. Come up with a plan and I'm game enough.'

'Oh, I know that, Gina.' Celia gave a long, mournful sigh. 'The trouble is, I can't think of anything at all to get us out of this situation. Come on, let's ride to the ridge.'

'That tree's got to come down,' Georgina murmured as they moved off, and Celia's bright blue eyes pinned her triumphantly.

'I knew you were working! You never stop.'

'Managing the estates is my job and I love it. I wasn't born with a silver spoon in my mouth.'

'You can have mine,' Celia muttered. 'At the moment it's choking me.'

They rode in silence for a while, walking the horses down to the valley floor and then slowly climbing to the high ridge. In late March it was cold and crisp, but neither felt it. For years they had ridden together on the Templeton lands. Celia had been born in the stately old hall and Georgina had come to the estate manager's house when she was five years old, a tiny, bright-haired child with enormous eyes, clutching her mother's hand as her father had taken over the Dower House that was to be her home from then on.

She had lived close to the Templetons and with the Templetons ever since and when her father retired she would take over the managing of the estate. She was trained for it, loved it. There was nothing else she wanted to do.

'Steven will think of something!' Celia suddenly announced, relief in her voice. 'He'll be here this week and he'll solve our problems. He always has done. Why didn't I think of it sooner? Oh, bliss!'

For a second Georgina stiffened, the cold she had not felt before rushing into her. Steven! He couldn't come back! He was banished from her mind, cast out, a traitor! A picture rushed into her head, a face harshly beautiful in a purely masculine way, eyes like sapphires, piercingly blue, hair as black as night. Steven, the deserter. She closed her eyes, forcing his image away. She would never trust him again, never in the whole of her life.

'I didn't know he was coming back.' It was wonderful to hear her own slightly husky voice so well controlled when she wanted to shout and rage, to gallop like mad—screaming.

'Daddy heard yesterday but, what with one thing and another, I forgot to tell you.'

'Why should you tell me?' Georgina managed a faint laugh of surprise. 'It has absolutely nothing to do with me at all.'

'Oh, come on, Gina! You were always Steven's personal problem, right from the time when your father became our estate manager. You probably spent more time at the hall than at your own home. Steven spoiled you right from the first. What did he call you? Sunflower—that's it.'

'Among other things,' Georgina said stiffly. 'I merely remember his bossiness.'

'Steven isn't bossy,' Celia insisted, glancing at her friend keenly. 'He's always been in charge, one way or another, and one day he'll inherit all this and more besides. Even as a child he was never allowed to forget his responsibilities both to the family and to the Templeton Estates, and he never has forgotten. He was always good to us all, including you.'

'I seem to remember a time when he put me over his knee and gave me a damned good hiding!' Georgina pointed out abruptly. She could remember other things too, but Celia idolised her brother and it was not up to her to point out his failings.

'Two hard slaps on the seat of your jeans can't be a good hiding, however annoyed you were,' Celia laughed. 'You were a little terror at nine and if Steven hadn't come you could have killed yourself. Let me remind you that you got in his car and took the handbrake off. You were heading straight for a wall.'

'With the possibility of denting his new car,' Georgina muttered angrily.

'With the possibility of denting yourself, you mean. Anyway, he hugged you better afterwards. I remember that perfectly well. There was only Steven who could handle you. We left him to it because you were a wild little thing, but, as I say, you were his particular problem.'

'Well, at twenty-two I can hardly be classified as a problem now.' The fierce tide of temper was beginning to flow and Celia looked at her quickly.

'You've got the same hot temper and the same red hair. Go easy on Steven, Gina. He's got one hell of a temper of his own,' Celia pointed out uneasily. 'We can't face any more trouble at the moment and we all adore Steven.'

'I can't think how I can cause more trouble,' Georgina bit out suddenly, her annoyance beginning to boil over. 'My name is Summers, not Templeton.'

For a second Celia looked stunned, and then the Templeton eyes flashed.

'Why, you wretch! You've always been like one of us. Steven had more say in your life than your father did. He even pulled rank to get you into the same school as me.'

'I never wanted to go to boarding-school!' Georgina fumed.

'No, because you couldn't face being away from Steve. I don't know why you turned against him finally, but I *did* notice. Don't keep up the feud or I'll never forgive you. We need all the help we can get with Auriel Delafield in our midst.'

For a second they glared at each other, Celia hotly defending her brother, Georgina too filled with memories to ease off, her volatile temperament clearly visible on her face, the long honey-coloured eyes sparkling. It didn't last long. They were too deeply attached to each other to battle, and at the same moment they burst into laughter.

'I'll try,' Georgina promised. 'Count on me. Let's get back. I've got jobs to do.'

'You know, I've been thinking,' Celia murmured, lingering a minute longer. 'You're really beautiful, especially when you're annoyed, those flashing eyes, the red hair. If you changed your image—er—rearranged yourself a bit we could at least have a bit of fun out of it.'

'What are you up to?' Georgina reined in sharply and looked with great suspicion at her closest friend.

'Auriel thinks she's the bee's knees,' Celia pointed out with a grim frown. 'All that gloss.'

'She's a model. Naturally she has gloss.'

'There's nothing natural about it. Strip her of that paint and you've got a barn door.'

'Not exactly,' Georgina grinned. 'What has all this got to do with "rearranging myself"?'

'*You're* beautiful, really beautiful!' Celia insisted. 'You're small, vivid, unusual. If you made an effort you would make her seem so shallow.'

'To what purpose?'

'Well, to give me a laugh for one thing. I can't remember when you last wore a dress and your hair is too long. That plait!' She grimaced, but Georgina only laughed.

'I'm a working girl.'

'And you look it. That female actually asked Mummy if you were a stable hand of one of the farm workers. I think she imagined you'd wandered in by mistake and we were too polite to ask you to leave. I thought Mummy was going to scream.'

Georgina burst into peals of laughter, but Celia frowned at her.

'It wasn't so damned funny. Mummy went all cold and dignified. She said, "*That* is Georgina. We are very fond of Georgina." Of course, you were sublimely ignorant of this little trauma. You went tramping out in your jeans and riding boots and I expect you went off to fell a tree. What's the matter with you, Gina? Just once in a while you could swirl by in silk. You look stunning dressed up but you just don't bother.'

'I like me as I am. However, I'll give it some thought.' Georgina turned Stardust away and led the way back, after a minute breaking into a fast gallop to ease her mind. She knew perfectly well why she didn't often bother. Celia had a selective memory. She didn't remember the brace that Georgina had had to wear on her teeth for two years, the embarrassment of it, Steven's amusement. Celia had never been called 'George' by her lofty brother. Celia had never been made to feel like a wild and rather ugly boy. Celia didn't know that her idol had a whole sackful of lady-loves.

As they finally walked their horses across the park Georgina felt the last of her temper drain away. Kellerdale Hall stood on a slight rise, overlooking the great sweep of parkland, and at the sight of it a feeling of well-being flooded through her in spite of everything. The gabled fronts stood proud of the stately house; great shining windows with ivy trailing between them caught the light of the morning sun. The front of the house was set slightly back with wide, shallow steps reaching an imposing carved door, the old wood black with age and weather.

Great copper beeches, oak and elm formed a backdrop to the tranquillity, banks of flowering shrubs softening the steep descent to the stretch of lawn. No formal gardens here, but space, grandeur, and Georgina knew from her lifelong love of the place and her attachment to this family that every window looked out on beauty. If she had to leave here she would never settle again anywhere. It was home, peace, all she ever wanted.

They rode round to the back, the horses walking in unison, sharp hoofs ringing on the cobbles of the stableyard, and at the sound the two men there raised their heads and smiled in greeting. The family likeness was all there to see, the Templeton height, the blue eyes, but neither had the striking presence of Steven Templeton. Malcolm's eyes were the clear blue of Celia's, not the piercing, startling sapphire of his brother's. His hair too was not that raven black, simply dark, and although he was handsome he did not have Steven's austere masculine grace.

Perhaps at one time Sir Graham Templeton had been almost as perfectly blessed as his eldest son, but he was no longer young, his hair white, and his expression softened as he saw the two girls. He was looking tired, Georgina thought with a pang. The straight back was not now quite as straight. One day Steven would face this burden. The full weight of the Templeton Estates would fall on his shoulders. He would be Sir Steven then, different.

It was something that had never entered her mind until today and an odd shiver passed over her skin. Sir Steven Templeton! Aloof, remote, unreachable. The white flashing smile that had softened her childhood, captured her teenage heart, seemed to come to mock her, and once again she thrust him from her mind. He had gone a long time ago, four years ago, and she had been glad to see the back of him. He was nothing to her at all.

'We were just discussing the future of this rare beast,' Sir Graham murmured, nodding towards the huge black stallion that watched with intelligent eyes as the two girls dismounted.

'Royal? He's a beauty,' Georgina remarked. 'Just so long as I don't have to ride him.'

'Terrifying thought,' Celia agreed. 'He only has to roll his eyes once at me and I'm off, even when he's safely boxed. I don't know why you wanted him, Father.'

'Breeding, my girl, as Georgina knows. I admit, though, that he's a handful. It takes Joe all his time to handle him.'

'That's true, right enough.' Joe Brissley, the head groom, walked up and took the two horses. 'I'll see to these, ladies, if you like. The stallion's a fine animal, Sir Graham,' he added as he led the horses away, 'but he puts the fear of death into everybody.'

'Well, Steven will be here soon,' Malcolm surmised, 'so I expect this brute will soon be tamed. He's been known to tame other things,' he added with a sly grin at Georgina. 'God knows why he went off in the first place. He could have let me go. I wouldn't mind a spell in Canada.'

'We have plenty of business outside this one estate,' Sir Graham pointed out gruffly. 'Steven has always spent time in Canada and in the States. As to going off for so long, he had his reasons. He always has good reasons.'

'Naturally. I never knew him not to be in charge of himself—and everybody else.' Malcolm's dry comment seemed to be lost on his father but Celia glanced across in sudden alarm.

'Mal! What's come over you? You dote on him as much as we all do, *and* rely on him.'

'True.' Malcolm gave his sister a rueful look. 'Bit of envy, perhaps?'

'Rubbish!' Sir Graham came out of his reverie and stopped staring at the stallion who seemed to be looking back at him arrogantly. 'Steven's the best friend you've ever had.'

'Agreed.' Malcolm's rueful look had changed to wry humour. 'Trouble is, he's the best everything.'

Georgina smiled when he looked at her but her own thoughts went on their separate dark pathway. Yes. The best everything. Supreme hero, supreme intelligence, supreme traitor. She felt a wave of pity for Malcolm. He was too nice, too kind, still in Steven's shadow. Steven had always been hero material, even as a boy, and now Malcolm had landed himself with Auriel. Everything was coming apart, and her own days at Kellerdale Hall, almost as one of the family, would seem to be about over. She knew her own character. A few more remarks from Miss Delafield and Georgina would blow up in her face and embarrass everyone.

Anyway, Steven was coming back so that was that. In future she would stay in her own home and try to remember that, as Auriel had subtly pointed out on at least two occasions, she was simply an estate worker, the daughter and right-hand man of the estate manager. It looked as if she was going to have to meet Celia by prior arrangement before long. Any forays into the hall and she was likely to encounter either the latest thorn in the flesh or Steven. Both were greatly to be avoided.

'Steven may decide to send you out to Canada, anyway, Malcolm.'

Sir Graham's remark drew Georgina rapidly back to the present. *Steven* may decide! He hadn't taken over yet. That was a nasty-looking bridge she would have to cross when she came to it, because she couldn't work for Steven. She looked intently at Sir Graham, a *frisson* of alarm running through her. He couldn't be thinking of retiring now and handing over, surely? Maybe his mind was wandering? That thought wasn't much comfort either and Georgina pleaded pressure of work and escaped, alarmed beyond words when Sir Graham called after her that there would be a dinner for Steven when he finally arrived.

Her shocked expression brought an amused grin to Malcolm's face and a very speculative look to Celia's. She had visions of Celia dressing her up in satin and lace to annoy Auriel. She had to get out of this celebration meal somehow. Naturally the fatted calf would be killed for the prodigal's return. How to escape the ordeal was Georgina's only problem. They had always included her in everything. It had to stop, even if it meant deserting under fire. She was very fond of Lady Evelyn, though, and she knew what a strain the arrival of Malcolm's fiancée had put on her.

Damn! She bit her soft lip in vexation as she trudged home. Why did things have to be so complicated? She hadn't seen Steven for four years. He hadn't made one visit home. There was no avoiding him now, though. It would look very bad if she refused to go to this dinner, and also her father would be grieved. He was always invited too.

Whatever Miss Delafield thought, an estate manager was not one of the workers. His standing was very high on the Templeton Estates and Georgina knew already that she could never quite fill his shoes when he retired. She could only try and hope fervently that Sir Graham would give her the chance. She hoped too that by the time Steven took over she would be a sour old spinster, too vinegary to be challenged. For the first time ever she looked around the estate with the possibility of an end to all this, her wonderful existence. It had seemed to be endless and now the storm clouds were gathering—first Auriel and now Steven. By the time she reached home she was sunk into gloom.

It was almost dark that evening when Georgina remembered the fencing at the Home Farm. During her ride with Celia she had noticed a whole section down but during the course of the day it had slipped her mind. If Jack Gregory didn't come out and do something about it there would be cattle on the lawn when Sir Graham got up tomorrow.

'Give Jack a ring,' Harry Summers suggested. 'I need you in the study for about an hour. The paperwork is piling up.'

'I can't just ring him, Dad. It's going to be dark soon. I had plenty of time to tell him earlier and I forgot. As it is, he'll have to turn out in the dark. I feel too guilty about forgetting. I'll tell him face on.'

'He should have seen it himself.'

'Well, he didn't. I'll just nip over.'

He followed her out, standing by her for a second to appreciate the garden. This was not Kellerdale Hall but it was beautiful in its own special way. The Dower House was not so old but it was still a pretty grand house. Of stone like the hall, clean-cut and pleasing, it stood in an acre of garden made specially private by high banks of rhododendrons and azaleas which would spring into wild colour later in the year.

Her father's pleased looks faded when she wheeled out her motorbike.

'You're not going on that? One of these days you'll kill yourself!'

'It's a good way of getting about. I only use it on the estate.'

'There are two Land Rovers by the gate. They're for getting about. As to that last remark, I saw you in the village with that bike the day before yesterday.'

'I only went to post a letter to Rowena,' Georgina wheedled. Her father never stopped grumbling about the bike. It was a Suzuki two-fifty, noted for its high revving, and he equated the noise with speed, even when she was only dawdling along.

'Why you were there is immaterial. You *were* there. I don't like that bike.' He glared for a minute and then gave in when she grinned at him impudently. 'How is Rowena, anyway?'

He was very fond of her old school-friend, and that had been a stroke of genius to silence him.

'Still round as a barrel, according to her. Merely plump to others. Apparently she's grown an inch and, being stretched longer, she's slimmed out a bit.'

Her father laughed and shook his head.

'She's a grand girl, Rowena. Invite her over—after you've got rid of that bike. She's as bad as you.'

It seemed to be the signal to go and Georgina swept out of the yard, trying to keep the revs down, trying to work out a suitable way of telling Jack Gregory about the fence. It was true he should have seen it himself but she hadn't acquired her father's way of giving orders and she doubted if she ever would. Maybe she wasn't suited to take his place when he retired? The thought filled her with horror. It would mean that they would have to leave the Dower House to a new manager. Buying another house would be no problem but it wouldn't be on the estate. No, she just had to follow in her father's footsteps. They *couldn't* leave here.

She whizzed down the narrow country road, banishing black thoughts. She would cut off across the field at the bottom of the lane. It would save time. Already a deepening dusk was settling on the landscape. Jack would have to go out with a lamp. Should she offer to help? No. Her father would be furious; so would Sir Graham if he found out.

She tore round the corner on the wrong side of the road and jammed on her brakes as she found the road almost filled with a fast sports car travelling towards her.

She heard the car brake too, but by then her bike was going into a skid and a million things seemed to race through her head. She had no helmet on, she would never see her father again, never see Kellerdale Hall, never ride across the hills...

The bike went one way and Georgina went the other, sailing through the air like a brightly coloured bird, light and slender, fearfully breakable, and it was funny how long it seemed to take. She saw sparks flying as the bike slid along the road and then every bit of breath left her body as she landed, not on the hard surface of the road but in the deep grassy ditch at the side.

The grass was not enough to cushion her fall very much. It was only inches deep and below it there was hard earth. She had been thrown from horses before and she knew how to fall, but her speed had been against her and the shock of the fall kept her quite still. She lay utterly motionless, her eyes closed, all the colour drained from her face.

She looked like a crushed flower, discarded by the wayside, and the man who sprang from the car and raced over to her was pale himself beneath a golden tan. He scrambled down beside her, running his hands over her slender limbs, relief etched on his face as he heard her breathing return to normal. A spasm of pain twisted her soft mouth, and when she opened dazed eyes her gaze was held, pinned by brilliant blue, sapphire blue, and she closed her own eyes quickly in a forlorn attempt at self-defence. Steven had come home.

'Open your eyes!'

His voice was the same as ever, dark, commanding, and as ever she obeyed automatically. So much for avoiding him! She could easily have landed on him and now she couldn't look away. For the tiniest second all grief and anger fled, her world filled with the dazzling blue of his eyes.

'Steven!'

'You little fool!' His voice rasped at her, cutting into her, dispelling the momentary joy, and she moved convulsively, escape uppermost in her mind. 'Lie still!' he ordered harshly, forcing her back. 'You damned near killed yourself.'

'I'm perfectly all right.' When she closed her eyes stars danced about, giddiness flooding through her. Her husky voice sounded weak. She could even hear it herself, and apparently he heard it too because his frown increased to near rage.

'I hope we're talking about your bodily condition and not your mental state. What the hell are you doing on a motorbike? Harry has some explaining to do,' he added with menace.

'I'm twenty-two,' Georgina pointed out, gazing up at him again.

'Chronologically only. In the head you've never advanced a year. Harry never could control you!'

He glared down at her and she was too dazed to retaliate. He was holding her still with hands that were more gentle than his tone suggested. If it hadn't been for that fact she would have thought he was contemplating strangling her.

A warm, rough tongue tested her cheek and Georgina turned her head slightly to see a huge black Great Dane bending over her solicitously. It licked the tip of her nose.

'The Hound of the Baskervilles. Hello, Prince, my sweet; you've aged.' She managed a shaky smile as it gave the well-remembered foolish grin, and Steven snapped at it ferociously.

'Get back in the car, you fool dog.'

'It's not his fault.'

'Oh, I've never had any doubts as to where to place the blame when you're around,' he muttered nastily.

'Let's get you in the car. You don't seem to have broken anything—astonishingly.'

'My bike!' She began to protest as soon as he lifted her but he was in no mood to listen.

'It can stay where it is in the opposite hedge, and if I ever see you on it again I'll take it apart piece by piece and scatter it over a twelve-mile area.'

'You'll do no such thing!'

'It was not any sort of request,' he growled. 'On this estate you toe the line.'

Or else… He didn't add anything but a dreadful threat was there and Georgina stole a glance at him. She had never seen him quite so annoyed, and counted it a good idea to keep silent for now. In any case he wasn't asking her opinion. He strode to the car and put her very carefully in the passenger-seat, almost snarling at Prince, who leaned forward to offer further first aid.

'I was on my way to the Home Farm,' Georgina managed in a small voice. 'There's a fence down. I have to tell Jack Gregory.'

'Tell him tomorrow,' he snapped, starting the car.

'The cattle will get out. I saw it earlier but I was busy and I forgot, so it's my fault.'

'The hell it is! Jack's supposed to be running the farm.'

'He runs it very well,' Georgina pointed out weakly. 'I can't see any reason for this rage either. I'm the injured party and I'm quite prepared to take the blame. I was on the wrong side of the road.'

He shot her a furious glance.

'Believe it or not, it rattles me when I run down a farmer's boy. I've never been able to manage it with the necessary equanimity.'

His blue eyes flared over her contemptuously from the long plait to the trousers and high boots. He was still scathing of her. She kept silent, suddenly rather tearful. Shock, of course. Her head rested against the luxurious upholstery of the seat—another Porsche, naturally. He was back, dark, splendid and sarcastic. He hadn't changed one bit.

'How do you feel?' he asked more quietly, the blue eyes lancing over her again. Her skin was perfectly white against her dark red hair and she was obviously in pain. She shut him out quite easily by closing her eyes.

'Very well, thanks. Quite ready for my evening jog.'

'Still the same idiot, George?' he enquired softly and she stiffened all over, actually hurting herself. He was here again to torture her. George. A farmer's boy. He would not rob her of confidence again. This time she would fight him.

'George is a boy's name,' she said bitterly.

'You want me to call you something gentle and old-fashioned? Amelia? It wouldn't fit. I don't know any girls who ride motorbikes.'

'Then you've missed out somewhere. Plenty do.'

'But not you, George. Never again,' he threatened. 'I've warned you. Sell the bike, give it away, or I'll smash it up.'

'You can't order me about!'

'We'll see,' he murmured quietly. 'Now calm yourself down and relax. You're only doing yourself damage.'

Nothing and nobody could damage her like Steven. It was astonishing how he could get her fuming with such speed. She glanced at his handsome profile and as quickly looked away. One look at Steven flung her headlong into the past, the painful past. She closed her eyes again, trying to reckon up where this put her. At least she had got over the hurdle of meeting him, even though painfully and at great personal risk. On the other hand, it had given him the chance to start ordering her about at once.

He had been quietly the boss since he was in his early twenties but this attitude was a little different. It mixed uncomfortably with her earlier thoughts and she really wanted to cry. Deep inside she knew it would all soon be over for her here. There was something about Steven that told her clearly. In any case, he liked her as little as she liked him. Four years had obviously not changed him. The contempt showed through.

CHAPTER TWO

GEORGINA protested when Steven pulled up at the Dower House and looked as if he was about to carry her indoors.

'I'm perfectly capable of managing.'

'Managing to do what?' He swung her up into his arms and even the movement of that made her light-headed. He noticed the way her teeth bit into her lip as she stifled a small exclamation of pain, but apart from a cold glance at her he ignored it as he was ignoring her. She was just some idiot he had been unfortunate enough to be mixed up with in the past.

'Is that you, Georgina?' her father called out on his way from the study, but it was Steven who answered.

'In a manner of speaking. I'm surprised at you, Harry. You should never have allowed a motorbike.' Steven was curt to the point of threat, and her father's surprised face showed round the door.

'My God! Is she hurt badly?' Harry Summers went quite pale and Steven relented very slightly.

'I don't think so, but we'd better get Bill Davis over here. Give him a call.' He was depositing Georgina on the settee and her father hurried to obey, picking up the phone and dialling for the doctor.

'She refuses to give up that bike, Mr Steven.'

'Why are you calling him that?' Georgina complained fretfully. It was just playing into his hands. Steven didn't seem to have heard. He was watching her, his eyes coldly blue. 'He's been Steven to you for more than sixteen years. Pretty soon you'll be touching your forelock.'

24

'He must be all of thirty-four or -five now,' her father explained vaguely, still listening for the doctor. 'One day he'll be Sir Steven.' She wondered if he too was rambling, and she didn't need to be reminded about the way that Steven would one day be remote. She wished he were remote now, about a thousand miles remote.

'Drop it, Harry,' Steven ordered curtly. 'I'll begin to think George inherited her insanity from you. And she'll not ride that bike again!'

'Maybe now you're here she won't,' her father agreed.

'I am twenty-two!' Georgina said loudly, struggling to get up and wincing at the pain. 'I shall do as I please.'

'*Not* while you work for Templeton Estates,' Steven informed her flatly. The blue eyes pinned her mercilessly until she subsided. She was very pale again and her lashes drifted down over her eyes. Tomorrow she would fight him. Tomorrow without fail. She couldn't manage it now.

'He's on his way,' her father announced, coming to look down at her anxiously. 'You'll be wanting to get up to the hall, Steven.'

'When I know the extent of the damage here. After all, I'm part of it.' He sat down and Georgina didn't need to open her eyes to know he would do exactly as he thought fit. Hadn't he always? Belatedly she remembered the cattle and tried to struggle up.

'I—I've got to let Jack Gregory know...'

Steven didn't even give her the chance to finish her statement. He was on his feet and snatching the phone up, punching the buttons impatiently, and she knew when Jack answered because Steven rapped out, 'You've got a fence down. We don't want cattle all over the front lawn. Yes, I'm back, and yes, you should have bloody well seen it yourself.'

He slammed the phone down and Georgina turned pained, reproachful eyes on him as she sank back to the cushions.

'Jack's a nice man. That wasn't either kind or diplomatic.'

'I don't have to be either!' He poured himself a drink without so much as a by-your-leave, and Harry looked from one to the other anxiously. Steven was back and people had better jump. Georgina had felt the last of the loose rein. Somehow he didn't think he would be seeing that bike again, not with Steven here. He glanced at his daughter as she lay with closed eyes.

She was beautiful, and sometimes, like now, she looked so small. At the moment she was creamy pale, her dark red hair making her face look paler still. She wasn't as tough as she thought. He moved forward to pull off her high boots, and Steven watched grimly, his mouth one tight line of temper. It was a rather uncomfortable moment for Harry because he could feel annoyance radiating through the air.

Georgina stayed out of it by keeping her eyes closed. Damn Steven! She was in an utter fix. She couldn't just fly at him, because it would simply upset the whole family. Anyway, one day he would employ her and she wasn't likely to take kindly to the thought if she set about him each time they met. It was obvious that he'd come back in the same frame of mind. She was still George, still an idiot. How could she ever have been devoted to such a man? So much for the renowned instincts of childhood. And so much for idiotic teenage crushes!

When Bill Davis came the whole procedure was repeated.

'Can't say I haven't been expecting this,' he confessed drily as he tested her limbs for breaks and her eyes for concussion. 'Tearing around on that bike...you're lucky to get off so lightly. Next time——'

'There won't be a next time,' Steven informed him grimly, staring down at her as if she were a displeasing biological specimen. Of course, he hadn't gone out during this examination, not that she was undressed, but the proprietorial attitude annoyed her—the lord of the manor bit. It was all right for her father to stay, but not Steven. It had nothing to do with him.

Bill Davis was old now, ready for retiring, and he seemed to think she was still a child. He should have firmly ordered Steven out but he hadn't. Even the local doctor bowed to Steven's dominance. To her way of thinking an older man like that should have been able to put his foot down, pull rank, even if it was only medical rank.

'Not much wrong,' he concluded finally. 'Bit of shock. Give her until tomorrow afternoon. If she's still all a-dither let me know.'

'I'm not dithering now,' Georgina pointed out crossly, glaring at him, and Steven looked down at her coldly in his superior fashion.

'Then spring up and go to bed.'

When she did she fell right over, but he caught her neatly, swinging her up into his arms.

'Hah!' Bill Davis frowned over his spectacles and then ignored her. 'Knows everything, doesn't she? Always did. Red hair. How about a drink, Harry?'

'It's about time he retired,' Georgina muttered heatedly as she was carried firmly to the stairs, her opinion never having been asked this time either.

'You fancy a handsome young doctor?' Steven asked drily.

'I don't fancy anyone. In any case, I'm going steady.' Which was a lie in a way. She frequently went out with Jeremy Ripley, who had a farm a few miles away from the Templeton estate, but it couldn't be classed as going steady. She had never seriously considered Jeremy. She supposed he was a calming influence, not at all volatile, and he never took anyone else out. All the same, she had never given him too much thought, even though she was fond of him. The estate was her abiding interest these days.

'Going steady? Yes, so I hear from Mother. Young Ripley, isn't it?'

'He's twenty-five!' Georgina glared up at Steven as he mounted the stairs, carrying her as if she were nothing heavier than a doll. He was utterly unmoved by having her in his arms, too, and that rankled in spite of her opinion of him.

'Really? One forgets. I remember him when he was a snivelling boy.'

'How condescending! I suppose you remember me when I was a snivelling boy too?

'You never snivelled, George.' He was laughing down at her suddenly, the blue eyes dancing, that devastating smile lighting up his whole face, and Georgina felt a great surge of feeling, almost beautiful memories from the past, from the time when she had adored him. There were other memories too and she wouldn't forget them.

'You shouldn't be up here, in my room,' she said sombrely as he casually shouldered her bedroom door open. Of course, he knew exactly where her room was. It wasn't the first time he had carried her up here, but then she had been a very tiny child.

'I guarantee not to attack you without written warning,' he murmured. The white smile flashed and she went hot all over, very anxious and restless.

'My father shouldn't have allowed this. He should have brought me himself. You're almost a stranger.'

'Almost. Give a few screams and see what happens.'

'I damned well know! He'll shout from the bottom of the stairs, asking you what I'm up to now.'

He just laughed and put her quite gently on the bed.

'Can you manage?'

'Thank you, yes.' She raised her head with a great deal of dignity, ignoring the pain, and he looked at her steadily before turning to the door.

'Crawl into bed, then. Goodnight.'

Just for a minute she felt quite mournful, desolate. Steven brought back so many memories, not all of them bad.

'Steven, are you staying? I mean—are you home for long?'

He stood at the doorway and looked at her levelly, the piercing blue eyes searching her face.

'For good, I think. Why?'

'It's a bit tricky. I hate you and it's awkward.'

'I know. Trouble is, George, your father is part of the way of things around here. Until he retires you're stuck with us.'

Her eyes went like saucers.

'But when he retires I'll take over his job.'

She got no reply at all to that. He simply raised one black brow and then he went out, closing the door, and her heart sank lower and lower. He would get rid of her and it didn't matter a jot whether his father was still alive or not. Steven always had the last word and he had no intention of letting her even try for the job. They would have to leave, go somewhere else, never see Kellerdale Hall again.

She managed to get ready for bed but there was nothing but misery inside her. Hadn't she known what it would be like when Steven came back? He had made an enemy of himself years ago. Anyway, he had almost killed her.

The new horror of the situation refused to allow sleep and, much as she willed black and harmful thoughts his way, little pictures from the past crept into her mind, fragmented scenes that had her tossing uneasily in her

bed. Always Steven's problem. That's what Celia had
said, and she could see them all now as they had been,
the hall shining in the sunlight of summer, the garden
pathways warm. Steven was there, his raven-black hair
gleaming.

At eight she had been tiny, her dark red hair already
long, flying loosely over her shoulders as she ran beside
the much taller Celia. They were hiding from each other
behind the thick hedges and Steven had come with his
father, their grown-up voices making her anxious.

'Hello, Celia. Hiding?' Steven had stopped and looked
down at his ten-year-old sister and got a glare from her
blue eyes.

'You've spoiled it, Steven! Now she'll find me.'

To hear her friend speaking like that to Steven was
horrifying to Georgina, even if Celia was his sister. Steven
was *twenty*! He was important and quite perfect. She
came out of her hiding-place before he ordered her out,
looking up at him with wide honey-coloured eyes, expecting trouble.

What a relief it was to see his white smile, the way
the piercing blue eyes softened. And what a shock when
he bent and lifted her up into his arms.

'Hello, Sunflower,' he said softly. 'We'd better call
this game a draw. I think I spoiled it.'

'It's not fair,' Celia complained as the two men went
on their way. 'I would have won. Steven's a beast.'

'He is not!' Georgina said fiercely. 'It was all an accident and Steven is wonderful. When I grow up I'm
going to marry him.'

Laughter had them both turning, and Georgina's
small, pretty face went red as she saw Steven and Sir
Graham still standing there, their grown-up faces highly
amused.

'And that's a promise,' Steven threatened, shaking his
finger at her. 'I'll hold you to that.' She just ran as fast

as she could but he was always her hero, so different from the sixteen-year-old Malcolm, who looked aghast at her antics and disappeared fast. Steven was her talisman, her saint, her dark god—until she found him out.

She drifted into a troubled sleep that was haunted by a panther, dark and fierce with brilliant blue eyes that could see through stone. It followed her to destruction and drove her out into a cold world.

Next day the expected invitation to the hall for Steven's 'Welcome home' dinner arrived from Lady Evelyn. Georgina was feeling quite all right but thought rapidly of using her accident as an excuse, until she noticed the postscript, 'If Georgina is unwell we'll put it off until tomorrow.' That neatly closed any loophole and there was nothing for it but to accept.

Her father had insisted that she take the day off, which left her with nothing to do but hang around the house and think. Inevitably she thought of Steven. It was a good word because Steven was that—inevitable, predestined. His place in her life had been firmly fixed since childhood, the great house across the park her second home.

After five years at the Dower House her mother had simply walked out and left them, without pity and without warning, shattering what had seemed to be a happy life. Georgina had been ten and it had been Steven who had found her curled up in the grass on the edge of the woods. He had said nothing at all, simply gathered her into his arms, wiped her tear-stained face and held her. It was what she'd needed—warmth, security—and he had always seemed to know, her beloved Steven.

She supposed her great romantic crush on him had started then because he was always there, calming her, rescuing her and even, at times, making excuses for her. Her world had revolved around him. The amused cruelty had come later, and with it the knowledge that he was not the god she had imagined. There were women in his life, plenty of them. He didn't belong to her at all.

Georgina moved fretfully around her room. The great crush had died abruptly and she didn't even want to think about *that* time. What about this dinner, though? Celia had given her pause for thought. Did she neglect herself? Jeremy didn't seem to think so. He always seemed quite proud to take her out.

She had a shower and examined her bruises, which were remarkably few, considering her astonishing flight through the air. Truth to tell, she did feel a bit shaken still. Sometimes shock lingered, or so Bill Davis had said. Her father had passed that message on very firmly and ordered her indoors when she'd got up.

She viewed herself dispassionately in the bathroom mirror. She wasn't exactly tiny. She was petite, a lovely figure in miniature, a creamy skin emphasised by her dark red hair that now swirled around her, well below her shoulder-blades. Celia was perfectly right. It should be cut. It used to be quite wavy but the length and weight pulled it down. She couldn't get it cut before tonight. Not that she had any chance whatever of outshining Miss Delafield. That had been one of Celia's stray hopes.

The phone rang and she slipped on her silky robe and went down to answer it. It was Celia.

'I didn't ring earlier in case you were still in bed. How are you?'

'Fine. And how do you know, anyway?'

'Steven. He was quite shaken, you know. He says he nearly killed you.'

'I was on the wrong side of the road,' Georgina pointed out fairly. She could imagine the way Steven had announced it at home, his sardonic contempt when he mentioned her bike. Miss Delafield *would* have been amused. 'Anyway,' she added, swallowing her dismay at the thought, 'Prince gave me first aid. He licked my nose.'

'Isn't he a fool?' Celia laughed. 'It's great to have him back around the house, following Steven and knocking things over. He scared Auriel to bits.'

'Steven?'

'No, idiot! Prince. She gave a little melodious shriek. It intrigued Prince. He went right up to her and actually growled for the first time ever. I think his spell in quarantine has sharpened him up.'

'How is your *bête noire*?' Georgina chuckled at the thought of Auriel's fright. She looked a bit scared on a horse too, although she rode each day to prove some deep-seated point of her own.

'Our *bête noire*! You're in this, Gina. Tonight I expect you to shine.'

'Nothing will shine except my bruises. In any case, it's too late. I don't feel up to going in to have my hair cut, and I've nothing special to wear.'

'I'll come over after lunch,' Celia announced, and put the phone down before Georgina could protest. She stared at it disconsolately and then got to her feet. With Celia on the warpath she had better go and inspect her limited wardrobe. In this mood, Celia was likely to cut the hems off any possible dresses just to see how they looked. It would be best to get her own thoughts in before the appointed hour. First she would make herself a mid-morning coffee.

When she turned from the phone Steven was standing in the drawing-room doorway and she nearly jumped out of her skin. It was a great shock, actually, because she hadn't heard him come in. There were no latches on the doors in this old house, just great big keys and bolts. They never locked the doors during the day and often not even at night, not in the Templeton stronghold.

She went quite white and he watched her grimly.

'Anybody could walk in here,' he accused, looking at her as if she were inviting intruders for sheer mischief, back to accusation right from the word go.

'Somebody did. You made me jump.' She gave him a honey-eyed glare but he remained unimpressed.

'Is that why you've gone so pale?'

'Why else? I feel quite wobbly really,' she added quickly, wondering if it might just get her off this dinner party at the last minute. He didn't consider that.

'Sit down. I'll make you a coffee.'

He really was the limit! He was behaving as if he had never been away at all, as if he had never hurt her so cruelly, and she rounded on him with flashing eyes.

'*I'll* make coffee! Look, I live here!'

'Good. Make one for me.' When she moved off huffily to the kitchen he trailed along behind her and she was aware of him every inch of the way. Steven gave out vibes and she picked them up always. Even as a child she had known when he would be there, felt his presence. His hold over her had been almost mystical.

He leaned on the edge of the kitchen table and stared at her grimly while she filled the kettle and got out cups. She felt about eight again and it was infuriating, this anxiety, as if he was just waiting to take her to task. He probably was!

'Large or small?' She turned on him defiantly, determined not to be browbeaten, and he looked back at her, completely unsmiling.

'It's a game and you never explained the rules. Is it behind your back? How many guesses do I get?'

'I'm asking if you want a large cup for coffee or a dainty little one,' she snapped, looking at him fiercely. His brilliant eyes were worrying her and she wished he would go and leave her in peace.

'Oh, large.' He still wasn't smiling and she looked away quickly, fighting down anxiety. Her hands were beginning to shake and the coffee-cups rattled however hard she tried.

'You're trembling.' She thought she heard a certain amount of satisfaction in the deep voice and she went on to the attack immediately.

'I told you I was wobbly. It was a very bad fall when you come to think of it. You nearly killed me.' She was proud of her huskily weak voice but all it got was a sardonic smile, the blue eyes narrowed.

'Good try, George. However, I know that you and Celia live almost permanently one at each end of a telephone, though I can't think she was helping you to get out of my homecoming dinner. There must be another plot thickening. Want to tell me about it before it gets you into trouble?'

'I keep my own counsel,' Georgina snapped. 'I do not get into trouble. I think you're mixing me up with a teenager you used to know.'

As soon as she said that she was annoyed with herself. It was nothing new to have her tongue running away with her but the subject of her teenage years was not a thing she wanted probing ever.

'You mean you've changed?' he enquired ironically. 'You look exactly the same to me, and then, of course, there's the motorbike. An adolescent craze.'

'I'm sure you must be right,' Georgina managed with icy dignity. 'However, I am not at the moment immersed in any schoolgirl plot. Set your mind at rest.'

She couldn't think why he was here and he was getting her all on edge. He didn't answer and he didn't come to get his coffee. She had to carry it across to him. Her hand shook so much that she spilled some over her thumb and slammed the cup and saucer down quickly on the table, muttering and putting her thumb in her mouth.

'Let me see.' Before she could protest he had her hand on his, his blue eyes angry. 'You're not safe to be let out,' he muttered crossly, and she snatched her hand away.

'I am grown up and in charge of my own life!' She glared up at him, so small that she had to throw her head back to manage it.

'So it would seem,' he rasped. 'What's the occasion? Waiting for Ripley?'

'What do you mean?' His anger stunned her; also his attitude. As far as she could see, she hadn't done very much to bring on this attack.

'Don't be coy, George. It sits badly on you. Last night you were the same idiot I've known for years—trousers, boots and a motorbike. This morning you're all alone and all keyed up, obviously waiting for some momentous event.'

'I've no idea what you're talking about.' She hadn't, either. The event that was taking place now was more momentous than she could cope with.

He reached out and grasped her shoulders tightly, jerking her to face him head-on.

'What happened to the plait?'

'I had a shower and then the phone rang and——'

'And you're wearing nothing at all under this robe. All silky-soft like a kitten.'

She went a fiery red, her heart almost hammering out of her chest, her eyes wild, and of course he took it for guilt.

'Ripley phoned and you're waiting for his arrival?' he grated, his eyes icy blue. 'Does it have to be in your own home? Couldn't he take you to the farm, or does his mother object? While you live on this estate——'

Georgina erupted into fury, red hair flying, tilted eyes flashing sparks.

'You arrogant, insulting pig! What right have you to come here and chastise me?' She fought to free herself of the restraining hands but they merely tightened to steel. 'Jeremy is not like you!' she spat out. 'He doesn't treat me like either an ugly boy or a free and easy tart.'

'Don't say that!' he snapped, shaking her.

'Why? You implied it.' She was panting with exertion, quite breathless, and he drew her tightly against him.

'Stop it, Georgina. You had a nasty shock last night and this is doing you no good.'

She gave a hysterical little laugh, tears flooding into her eyes.

'It really is astonishing how I manage to come out worst every time. I was in my own home, minding my own business, and you appear like the devil you are, throwing accusations at me, and it's *my* fault. The only shock I've had is seeing you again. Get out of here!'

'I apologise.' He looked down at her with brilliant eyes. 'It incensed me to think you were waiting for Ripley like that.'

'Maybe I am. Maybe I'm lying.' Suddenly she was tired and trembling, and she turned away, only to be pulled back ruthlessly. For a second blue fire was flashing in his eyes again, but he saw her hastily blinked-away tears and his hold slackened.

'Drink your coffee.'

'I don't want it now.'

'Of course you do.' He pushed her into a chair at the table and handed her cup across. 'Drink it up and then go back to bed.'

'You can't tell me what to do.'

'I've been telling you what to do all your life,' he reminded her grimly. It brought to mind what a burden he must have found her and her face flooded with colour all over again.

'Not for four long years. You went away and I grew up. I'm qualified, efficient and single-minded.'

'Really?' He leaned against the table with his drink, sipping it and looking at her steadily. 'What are you single-minded about exactly——working?'

It sounded a bit threatening and she remembered his look of the night before. She wasn't going to let him know how much she feared that he would get rid of her.

'Working? Not really, although I enjoy it. Actually, I'm pretty single-minded about marriage.'

'Ripley?' His eyes narrowed and she nearly lost her nerve. 'Is he the one, or one of many?'

'I'm quite faithful,' Georgina breathed romantically. There was enough with one traitor on the estate.

'Are you?' His eyes were searching her mind and she knew perfectly well he could look through stone. Her heart went from hammering to erratic fluttering when he moved her cup and reached out for her, pulling her to her feet and into his arms. 'Let's see how faithful you are. Kiss me instead of Ripley.'

'I—I don't kiss just anybody. I'm no longer a child.' There was panic on her face and he smiled derisively. She was trembling and it seemed to give him a good deal of cruel satisfaction.

'You were no longer a child the last time I kissed you. You went into a state of sensual rapture.'

And that was what she would never think about, something that haunted her dreams, her own personal nightmare and disgrace.

'Let me go!' She stiffened, making herself tight and hostile, but he simply ran his hand down her back, warm against the silk, until she gasped and looked at him with more pleading than outrage.

'Not yet,' he murmured. 'I'm back, Georgina.'

'And—and I'm fair game?'

It hurt really badly. She knew all about his women. She had known a long time but he had always been her friend until those last few days.

'Why not? You're conveniently close by, and, in any case, I taught you everything you know. You can compare this with Jeremy's ardour.'

There was no comparison. None. He pulled her head to his shoulder and tilted her face, looking into her frantic eyes for a second before his lips closed over hers. Nobody had ever kissed her like that before, nobody but Steven that night when she had been eighteen. It had been her permanent downfall because nothing compared to Steven's kisses, the way he held her.

She seemed to be falling, spinning like a leaf, her breathing shallow, inadequate, and still he held her implacably, his mouth moving over hers, searching for more and more response until her legs just gave way and she sank completely against him.

'Please, Steven!' When he lifted his head a little she begged, and he looked down at her mockingly, holding her still, tightly against him.

'You said that before, too, but you weren't pleading to be free.'

It brought back all the humiliation, the great, deep shame, and she pulled free, forcing her trembling legs to hold her upright.

'I hate you!'

'No, you don't,' he said remorselessly. 'I'm an addiction for you. I always have been. From child to woman, you're still hooked. Quite obviously mine.'

'You conceited brute! Why are you doing this?'

He raised one devastating black eyebrow.

'Why not? I like to know you're there if I want to reach out for you, George.' That just about did it and she reached for the hot coffee. His hand slapped down over hers too quickly, though.

'I wouldn't,' he warned softly. 'Knowing you, you'd miss and I would retaliate quite violently.'

'If you touch me again I'll tell your mother,' she threatened wildly, and he threw back his head and laughed at her, clearly greatly amused.

'You're still weird. I'm thirty-four years old, as Harry rightly surmised.'

'Old enough to know better! So much for good breeding. Kindly leave.'

'Doesn't Jeremy lose his head and kiss you into a trance, then?' He settled himself against the table and proceeded to sip his coffee again, his eyes narrowed over her.

'Jeremy is not like you,' she said, pointing to the door. 'We have a perfectly smooth relationship.'

'Did you say "boring"?'

'I said *leave*!' she shouted, and he grinned at her widely before walking to the door.

'If you don't come tonight, George, I'll drive down and fetch you,' he threatened, and she glared at him, her own weakness forgotten, only his past and present crimes churning round in her mind. She pulled her robe tightly around her and raised her chin proudly.

'I would never let your mother down. I'm very fond of her, and Celia is my best friend.'

'And I'm your worst enemy? Come as you are, George. You look wildly feminine. Quite fit to eat.'

'*Go!*' She looked at him ferociously and he went. She could still hear him laughing as he got into his car, but by that time she had collapsed on to a chair, her legs finally refusing to move.

Celia came in the early afternoon, and Georgina had somewhat recovered—at least, her breathing was back to normal so long as she didn't think about it. She had tied her hair back in a bunch, and Celia came in very purposefully.

'That will have to go for a start,' she announced with just a slight tinge of her brother's forcefulness. 'I've brought my scissors.'

'Are you quite mad? You're not cutting my hair!' At that moment she had had quite enough of the Templeton pressure.

'Stop that panicky noise,' Celia ordered. 'I'm going to trim the ends. I've no intention of doing any topiary. I could never manage a peacock, even with this thick hair.'

'You're as bad as your brother,' Georgina complained, and Celia stopped for a second, interested.

'Steven? Has he been here?'

'No!'

'I see. When did he come?'

'This morning.' Georgina found her cheeks flushing, and Celia looked at her closely through the mirror.

'So, the battle continues?'

'To the death,' Georgina said through gritted teeth.

'I expect you're in love with him,' Celia surmised comfortably. 'It was only to be expected. I'd like you for a sister-in-law.'

'Get rid of Auriel and I'll have a shot at Malcolm.' Georgina felt really exasperated. The family had a smooth way of expecting to get everything they wanted. If she didn't love them so much they would irritate her beyond words.

'Sarcasm does not become a lady. Mother says so. Malcolm could never control you. He's too sweet.'

'Then count me out. And I'm no lady, according to your big brother. I'm an idiot.'

'Well, he's very fond of you. That gives him the right to say what he likes.' Celia peered at her. 'I'd like to cut you a fringe but I don't think I've quite got the skill.'

'You have no skill at all with hairdressing,' Georgina yelped as the scissors flashed. So Steven had the right to say what he liked? Really! What was she doing mixed up with the Templetons anyway? Right at this moment Celia was as bad as her brother. She ducked her head away.

'Have some faith, do,' Celia hissed. 'And hold still. Tonight I'm going to get a bit of "own back". Auriel is now after Steve.'

'What?' Georgina went quite still and Celia nodded her satisfaction.

'I thought that might interest you. It appears that she knew him before. In London. She's now buttering him up. If at first you don't succeed . . . et cetera. So far, Mal seems to be ignorant of the nuances. Steven is being quite polite. Mummy is anxious and I'm furious. *You* will restore the balance by turning her green.'

'I can't do anything.'

'We'll see,' Celia murmured, and Georgina just sat still and let her snip at the ends of her deep red hair, hoping for the best but too stunned by the news to really protest.

Had Auriel been the woman in London? She knew when he'd left he was going to one. Hadn't he told her so? Part of his cruel taunting when he pointed out that at eighteen she was still a child.

'I don't think I'm coming,' she muttered miserably.

'You are. If you don't I'll fetch you.' She would have to move fast. Steven had already threatened that and he was neither slow off the mark nor heavy on patience.

'I've nothing to wear.'

'Then we'll alter something you have. When you feel well we'll have a trip to town and rig you out splendidly. I know you never spend anything on yourself. You've probably got sacks of money stowed away. You can spend it.'

'It's for my old age,' Georgina protested wryly.

Celia picked up her hand and looked at the palm.

'You will marry a rich man, have lots of children with red hair and vividly blue eyes. You will live in a stately home. I see a big black dog.'

'And I see a mad fortune-teller. However, I'll mention all this to Jeremy. Unfortunately, his eyes are brown.'

'That lets him out, then,' Celia said crisply. 'Show me your wardrobe.'

As it turned out she had a beautiful caftan that she had never worn.

'What's this, then?' Celia pounced on it and Georgina had to explain that she'd bought it on impulse to attend a dance with Jeremy.

'And?'

'In the end I thought better of it. It was a sort of farmers' do. I went in the obligatory cotton frock and even that brought frowns to Mrs Ripley's face.'

'Jeremy's mother doesn't like cotton dresses?'

'Not with a scooped-out back. Too daring.'

Celia giggled and brought the caftan out. It was the colour of milky coffee, the hem patterned with autumn leaves. Against Georgina's red hair it looked perfect.

'You paid a lot for this,' Celia surmised suspiciously. 'I hope you're not serious about Jeremy Ripley?'

'I shall probably marry him!' Georgina snapped, remembering Steven's taunts.

'What a mistake. Jeremy is too tame by half. Let's get the heated rollers into that hair,' she sighed. 'Tomorrow you can go to the hairdresser's, but tonight we'll improvise. And, Gina, there's no going back after this,' she warned darkly. 'Riding boots are for riding, jeans are for work, and at all other times you will wear clothes. I will not have you inadequately dressed.'

The remark made Georgina blush suddenly, but fortunately Celia was busy with the heated rollers she had brought. This morning she had been very inadequately dressed. It made her remember Steven's arms around her and a shiver ran right over her skin. She had to be mad! He was good at things like that, as good as he was at everything else. He had probably kissed hundreds of women senseless. It infuriated her, especially when she recalled how he had gone off laughing. Did he imagine he was going to amuse himself with her while he was up here? She was no longer gullible. He would have to be taught a severe lesson.

CHAPTER THREE

As GEORGINA got ready for the homecoming dinner she felt scared. She had thought she could shrug off Steven easily but he had already proved she could not. She walked to her bedroom window and looked across towards the hall. It gleamed with lights, a sight she was so used to, but tonight there was fright and excitement inside to more than match the pleasure it gave her to look across at the old house.

Four years ago it had looked like that. It had been late summer, the gardens still smelling sweetly, alive with flowers, and Steven had taken her out to dinner, not even inviting Celia and Malcolm along. To her it had meant something, some commitment on his part, because he had been treating her differently.

School was all over and she was at college. He never came to see her, not as he had done when she was at school. With a flat in London he had always managed to be present on special days, taking her out with a few friends, but they were schoolgirl dreams and she had kept her feelings strictly under control, knowing he was a grown man and simply kind, her friend and protector, almost like a guardian.

At eighteen it was different. She felt like a woman and he treated her like one, courteously, gently. He had danced with her too, his arm tightly round her. At one point she had been sure that his lips had brushed her hair, although when she had looked up with wide dreamy eyes he had simply smiled and asked if she was tired.

She wasn't tired, she was entranced, and he had parked the car at the hall and then walked home with her, across the lawns and down the gravelled drive to her house.

'Oh, look!' The moon swam into sight through a perfect sky and Georgina stopped by the fence, wanting to share the beauty with Steven and not wanting to leave him and go home.

'There's a barn owl.' She pointed to the wide-winged flight of the owl against the moonlight.

'I see it.' He stood close to her, very patient and amused.

'It's rare to see one nowadays,' she got out breathlessly. 'At—at first I thought it was a bat.'

'After this glorious hair?' She had brushed her wavy hair into shining clouds, and it gleamed in the moonlight. She felt beautiful for the first time ever, and his brilliant blue eyes seemed to acknowledge it tonight. His hand stroked down her hair, his eyes following the movement, and she swayed towards him, her face filled with longing.

'Georgina!' It was a reprimand, his hands tight on her slender shoulders, holding her back, and she trembled in the warm night air, devastated by his tone.

'What did I do? I'm grown up, Steven. Don't you want to kiss me goodnight?'

'The way your boyfriends do? I'm not one of them,' he said harshly.

'I know.' She hung her head in shame, tears in her eyes. 'And—and they don't kiss me—not really.'

'How foolish of them,' he taunted. 'What a missed opportunity.'

'I—I won't let them kiss me properly. I don't like it.'

'Do you expect me to believe that? You just invited me to kiss you.' He sounded angry and he tilted her face to the moonlight, his face softening when he saw the tears on her cheeks.

'That's different,' she whispered unhappily. 'I belong to you, Steven.'

'Don't say that.' His hand cupped her face, his fingers wiping her tears.

'It's true!' More tears spilled to her cheeks, glittering like diamonds in the light, and he pulled her into his arms, his hand in her hair.

'Don't cry, Georgie,' he murmured. 'You'll grow up. You'll recover from this.'

'I am grown up and I don't want to recover,' she choked as he looked down at her for a moment as if torn in two ways.

'Be sensible,' he murmured, his eyes lancing over her tragic face. 'It's the moonlight, the romantic night. You're eighteen and just beginning to be a woman.'

'Isn't it sensible to be honest? I don't really have to tell you I belong to you, Steven. You already know.'

Tears glittered in her eyes and his face tightened, his fingers suddenly biting into her soft skin. She thought he was angry, because his face was taut, unsmiling. At any moment she expected harsh words of correction, but he pulled her closer, surrendering to a masculine impulse to conquer as his lips covered hers.

It was meant to be a kindly kiss, or even a warning—she had known that instinctively, but flame shot through her instantly and she felt him stiffen with shock before he tightened his arms and tilted her face, his mouth parting hers hungrily.

Within seconds she was wrapped in desire, moaning with pleasure. She could feel Steven's heart pounding over her own, his breathing uneven. Once for an instant he pushed her away but his hands seemed to be unable to stop reaching for her and she was back in his arms, his kisses like fire against her neck and cheeks, his murmurs of encouragement mingling with her small pleas to love her.

When he began to stroke her willing body she curled against him, her slender fingers in his thick hair. Joy was racing through her. She was Steven's at last. Now he would claim her as his own, marry her. She would always be with him.

It was a cold shock when he held her away, looking at her with blazing eyes.

'Enough, Georgina. I'm taking you home.' He sounded almost bitter, and she stared up at him with wide eyes.

'Will you come for me tomorrow?'

'Tomorrow I'm going to London. I'm taking over the office there.'

'You—you mean you're not coming back?' Her face was tragic and he turned away impatiently.

'Not for some time.'

'But what about us, Steven?'

'Us?' He turned back to her harshly at her horrified little whisper. 'There is no ''us'', Georgina! You're a child. I helped to rear you and now you've almost made it to maturity. I think I've borne the burden admirably so far, don't you?'

She recoiled as if he had struck her. She was still trembling from his kisses and he was perfectly normal, perfectly cold.

'You made love to me. I'm not a child.'

'I did not make love to you! I kissed you on your birthday after an agonised plea. It was my last effort in teaching you. Now you can ride, dance, swim and kiss. That lets me out.'

'There's a—a woman in London?' she asked shakily, suddenly remembering his long absences there for the past few years.

'A real, grown-up lady,' he agreed cruelly. 'You're eighteen with a long way to go. To me you're a child still. Stop dreaming foolish dreams, Georgina. Make your own life. One day you'll find just the person for you.'

She just turned and ran blindly, tears streaming down her face, not caring where she was going, fighting wildly, when he caught her and swept her off her feet.

'Stop it!' he ordered sharply. 'You have never had control over your emotions in your whole life. If you go mad whenever anyone kisses you you'll end up in trouble.'

No, she wouldn't. Nobody made her feel like that but Steven. She was quiet and sombre, refusing to look at him as he took her to the door, refusing to answer when he said goodbye. He was going to a woman and she felt her life was over at eighteen. He had kissed her like a lover and it had meant nothing at all to him because he already had a woman in London. She cried all night and in the morning she hated him, remembering nothing but the bad times. As far as she was concerned, Steven didn't exist.

Now he was back and she was going to his homecoming dinner, but now it was different. She knew what he was—hadn't he proved it this very afternoon? She would humiliate him if she could.

She learned a lot at the homecoming dinner and she didn't even have to try. It was pushed right under her nose. Kellerdale Hall was ablaze with light, every downstairs window glowing amber, and Georgina was anxious, fluttery inside. Nothing was the same and she knew that the feeling was coming from her own tightly stretched nerves. She was suddenly intensely aware that she was part of a plot and, though it had been aimed at Auriel, it now seemed to have subtly changed. Steven was involved and, although she wanted to teach him a lesson, one just did not make plans about Steven. He was too

powerful. All this was asking for trouble and she knew
it. Celia was crazy to think she could get away with it.

Georgina arrived with her father. He was quite re-
splendent in a dark suit, but then he was a handsome
man even at his age and she was always immensely proud
of him. She stuck to him like glue because she felt agitated, apprehensive. Things were no longer quite the
same. She didn't feel comfortably at home tonight and,
in any case, she was 'dressed to kill', as Celia had put
it, and that in itself was unusual.

Her thick long hair had taken to the heated rollers
beautifully, its natural wave all back. The fringe idea
discarded, Celia had arranged it parted down the middle
and teased off her face, and now it actually glowed in
the lights, changing from mahogany to red to gold as
she moved. With just the lightest make-up, her creamy
skin looked beautiful, her eyes cleverly emphasised until
they seemed to almost fill her small, lovely face. The
caftan was also a howling success, drifting around her
slender figure, silky and alluring, and Lady Evelyn was
delighted. She sailed across to greet them, clearly grateful
for reinforcements.

'Harry! It's so good of you to come. Georgina, my
dear, you look *beautiful*!'

Of course, it brought all eyes to them, and she was
nervously aware that brilliant blue eyes raked her from
head to foot although Steven merely smiled and nodded
in their direction.

'Look at her! Just look!' Celia detached Georgina
from her father and hissed into her ear, but Georgina
had already noticed Auriel firmly attached to Steven's
side. Every time he moved she moved with him.

'She's been like that since he came home,' Celia muttered angrily. 'Anyone would think she was pasted to
him. It's quite blatant. Outrageous! Mummy is so
embarrassed.'

But what encouragement was Auriel getting? That was what Georgina wanted to know. Had it been Auriel he had gone to when he'd left four years ago? If so, what had happened that she was now engaged to Malcolm? She was certainly a striking woman. A society girl turned model, as Celia had informed her. The blonde hair was not the natural cool blonde of Celia's but it was beautifully done, piled on her head like a confection, her tall, slim figure showing off a very expensive black lace dress.

'She looks a wow,' Georgina murmured fairly. 'She looks naturally elegant. It makes me feel as if I'm in fancy dress.'

'A hard-faced disgraceful wow,' Celia snapped under her breath. 'Just remember she's your target. *You* are the most beautiful thing here tonight. You've got youth and beauty. You're sexily lovely. And stop blushing. It's not sophisticated.'

'And can't be controlled to order. Stop your remarks and I'll stop blushing. Just let me pretend that things are quite normal.'

'Well, they're not.'

Georgina could only agree with that. She caught sight of herself in a mirror and almost gasped. She had never looked like this before in her life. Even with close inspection it didn't seem to be her. Her eyes were filling her face, slightly panic-stricken, as if she were just about to flee. She couldn't see anything even remotely sexy about herself, and that was a great relief.

Steven came up behind her and handed her a drink, his intent vivid blue eyes holding her startled reflection.

'It's champagne, George,' he told her quietly. 'Think you can take it?'

'I can take anything.' She swung round to face him defiantly and he smiled down at her.

'I'm beginning to think you can. Obviously you've matured under Ripley's care. What a pity he isn't here when you look so beautiful. Never mind. Count on me.'

'Ha!' She took the glass and had a good drink. 'Counting on you is something I definitely grew out of. I can't think why I ever did rely on you. You don't look particularly trustworthy. Now that I'm grown up, of course, I can see it.'

'This is my homecoming dinner,' he warned softly. 'If you're about to make one of your scenes, forget it.'

'I do not make scenes. As to this dinner, I'm prepared to be polite. That's as far as it goes.'

'You will sit by me at dinner.'

'I'll sit where your mother says!'

'And, knowing you're not to be trusted, she's placed you by me.'

She glared at him, wide-eyed, ready to do battle.

'Are you saying I'll make an exhibition of myself?' she enquired haughtily.

'Only if I kiss you. We'll keep off that tonight. I don't want the family to know about your sexual ecstasy. Do you realise, George, that I've only ever kissed you twice, and both times you've been more than willing? It does make one wonder about your regular behaviour.'

There wasn't a lot of subtlety in that and she should have known she would get the cruel lash of his tongue if she tried to defend herself. She didn't get the chance to answer back because, in the first place, she blushed painfully, confirming his worst fears, and, in the second place, Malcolm came up with Auriel.

'Georgina, you look beautiful. I'm stunned.' He kissed her hand with a great flourish and had her laughing straight away. Malcolm hadn't been away for four years. She was comfortable with Malcolm.

Auriel wasn't laughing.

'Why, of course, it's the little girl from the estate. I didn't know you without your plait.'

'It's detachable,' Georgina said brightly. 'I left it in the bathroom.'

Luckily the dinner gong went and Steven took her arm in a very firm grip, turning her away from Malcolm's laughter and Auriel's cool outrage.

'Behave yourself, George,' Steven murmured, clamping her to his side.

'I will not be put down!' she spat.

'My, my, my. I'll turn that one round in my mind for a while. In the meantime, behave beautifully. You look tiny and luscious. It would be a shame to spoil the illusion. This is twice in one day that you've stunned me.'

'I want to tell you something,' she muttered, smiling brilliantly at Lady Evelyn and getting a very grateful look. 'I just don't like you at all.'

'Tell me that again when there's nobody else in sight,' he threatened, tightening his hold to pain. 'You have definitely developed possibilities.'

'W-what do you mean?' Her heart suddenly lurched with fright and Steven gave her a slanting look that scared her even more.

'Surely you've dressed up to impress me? I never had trouble reading your mind and, as to Celia, she's not at all as clever as she thinks. I noticed the satisfied looks as you came in. I also noticed mother's little start of surprise as the goose turned out to be a swan. I naturally conclude that this is for me. Thank you, George. I appreciate it.'

He handed her courteously to her seat and she was glad to see Celia at the side of her, even if she did have to have Steven at the other side. Malcolm and Auriel sat opposite, and Auriel watched her with cold, glittering eyes as black as coal. Lady Evelyn looked almost poised for flight, and at the other end of the table her father and Sir Graham had already started a deep discussion about the fifty-acre field.

She might have known that Steven would notice the ploy. Nothing much fooled him. And what had he meant about her developing possibilities? She was trembling so much that she didn't know how she was going to eat. Had he asked his mother to sit her next to him?

'I take it you've left things in good hands in Canada, Steve?' Malcolm enquired as they ate the first course.

'The best, and of course Arnold Lang has taken over in London. I had to stay there for a while until everything was on an even keel. I can now settle down here.'

Georgina's spurt of feeling at that was never allowed to develop.

'So *that's* where you disappeared to? Canada!' Auriel put in with a seductive smile. 'I was just thinking. It's ages since you and I sat down for a meal together, Steven.'

There was an instant, subtle change in Malcolm's expression. Georgina thought he looked 'saddened to death'. Celia's shoulder nudged hers but she looked steadfastly at her own meal, finishing the melon and pushing the cherries around aimlessly. So it was true. It had been Auriel, and something had split them up. She didn't know why it should dismay her but it did.

'Does this mean that I'm second choice?' Malcolm asked with a rather bizarre attempt at humour. To everyone's dismay, Auriel didn't answer. She just looked at Steven and his eyes glinted like icy chips.

'Well, does it?' Steven asked in a hard voice and even Auriel blushed.

'Of course not! What a thing to say. I'm engaged to Malcolm. You disappeared and missed out.' She couldn't seem to resist the coy addition, and Steven shrugged, a sort of cold rebuff that was not at all his usual manner.

'I'm sure I'll survive.'

He was annoyed. Had he expected Auriel to remain faithful? Had this engagement been a great shock to him? Georgina wanted to get up and leave. She felt almost ill. Malcolm looked stunned and there was a silence around the table that had never happened before at the hall. Two brothers, rivals for the same woman! Georgina began to tremble. She couldn't seem to stop chasing the cherries around her plate, her eyes not even seeing them. Was Steven going to pass his time with *her* to take his mind off Auriel?

Steven leaned over and jabbed the cherries with his desert fork, eating them.

'What a thing to do!' Auriel gave a sort of hysterical laugh, and it *had* seemed a very intimate familiarity—even Georgina was startled.

'Georgina doesn't like cherries in port but she's too polite to say,' Steven remarked coolly. At least he wasn't calling her George at the table. She supposed she had to be grateful for that, even if he had drawn attention to her so blatantly.

'But to eat them . . . I mean!' Auriel couldn't seem to leave it alone and Celia pounced, missing no chance.

'Gina has always been Steven's girl. He covers up for her every time.'

'I see. A family pet.' Auriel's smile was as sweet as cyanide, and Celia was ready for that too.

'No. Just Steven's pet.'

Georgina felt as red as the cherries but she dared not say a word. She hadn't realised that Celia's bit of 'own back' would run to this. At any rate, Malcolm was not now so grim-looking and Lady Evelyn was smiling again, so maybe it was worth the embarrassment. Maybe too it made Steven feel less bitter about seeing his brother with the woman he wanted.

'Eat your fish, pet,' Steven said in a sarcastic whisper, and she bristled with rage. Was she about to be the scapegoat? No way! She didn't care if Steven was heart-broken. He probably knew exactly what Celia was up to. Nothing escaped him. She hoped Celia realised it. Wonderful big brother was a cad.

The rest of the evening turned out to be quite pleasant because Auriel was just a bit subdued and Celia counted it a small victory, as she pointed out to Georgina in a satisfied whisper later on. Georgina was well aware of Steven's sardonic gaze constantly on her and hadn't the slightest doubt that he knew exactly what had been planned. Of course, Celia blamed Auriel, but Georgina blamed Steven. A traitor to his brother, even. He just took everything he wanted. If Auriel went on like this then Steven would no doubt be prepared to walk off with her. She sipped at her champagne until she felt quite giddy.

It was Steven who put a stop to it, taking her glass and downing the drink at one go.

'That's enough for you,' he ordered drily. 'Your eyes are going crossed.'

'I'm not a child!' She made a grab for her glass and her long sleeve fell back, revealing the already darkened bruises that seemed to be rapidly spreading.

'Hell!' Steven grabbed her arm before she could cover it and inspected her minutely. 'How many more of these have you got?'

'Quite a few. They seem to be increasing by the hour.'

'Maybe you should see Bill Davis again.' He looked deadly serious for once, almost concerned, and Georgina, already hazy from the champagne, swayed a bit. He pulled her tightly to his side.

'Shall I take you home?'

'No fear.' She looked up at him with luminous eyes. If he was about to dangle her in front of Auriel she wasn't playing at all. 'In future I protect myself.' She got the old, lazy smile.

'Whoever hurts you, George, it won't be me.'

'I have bruises to refute that statement,' Georgina pointed out sharply, waving her arm in front of him just as Auriel came up quickly, catching the end of the sentence.

'Goodness! How did you get those?' she asked a little shrilly, her eyes flicking from one to the other of them.

'Steven did it. I've got bruises all over. He's a fiend when roused,' Georgina trilled in an alcoholic haze, and Auriel looked quite sick. It dawned on Georgina that maybe the *bête noire* hadn't heard about the accident after all. She opened her mouth to expand on the theme but Steven was too quick for her.

'Cool it!' he warned coldly. 'I'm taking you home.'

'Nobody asked you,' Georgina snapped, and Auriel looked more annoyed than ever.

'Does she always behave like this?'

'Rank hath its privileges,' Georgina smiled as Steven almost dragged her away. 'Being Steven's girl gives me a few perks. He'd let me do just about anything.'

'You're surely asking for it,' he muttered. 'I'm taking her home, Harry,' he announced as they came abreast of her father. 'Yesterday is catching up with her.'

'I'll be along soon,' her father promised vaguely. He had no idea how much in danger she was with Steven, and he ignored all her frantic little signals. Celia was grinning all over her face and Malcolm was looking suspiciously at everyone.

'I hope you'll be better tomorrow, dear,' Steven's mother said worriedly, pecking at Georgina's cheek. 'Thank you so much for coming when you didn't feel well. It was so good of her, wasn't it, Steven?'

'Angelic. She never fails to surprise me.' His mother smiled happily but there was ice deep in his voice that Georgina didn't miss. Right at that moment she would have just run off home by herself, but Steven's grip was bruising. There was no escaping him and she knew better than to try.

In the car her alcoholic euphoria suddenly left her, and she was a little nervous about being alone with Steven. There was a tension about him, anger racing underneath like an approaching storm. Even so, she wouldn't let him frighten her.

'This is twice my father has thrown me to the wolves,' she complained frostily.

'Wolf,' he corrected curtly. 'Me. That's how you see me, isn't it, Georgina?' He must be annoyed to be calling her that, because there was nobody else there, and she shot a worried glance at his starkly handsome profile, not too sure about her own bravery. All the same, she had to say something.

'You knew her before,' she accused. 'She was your mistress. Malcolm is devastated.'

'And, of course, I've always robbed him of everything? Surely you can see that he's robbed me? I had her and now he's got her.'

His acknowledgement of the truth shook her deeply but she would not let him know.

'You're better at everything. It's so unfair. If he's getting one over on you, if he sneaked in when you were in Canada, then it serves you right. Anyway, it's none of my business,' she suddenly choked, misery washing over her.

'It isn't,' he snapped. 'Keep quiet, therefore. With a bit of luck I'll have you home in five seconds.'

'And you're not coming in!'

'I don't waste my time with idiots,' he rasped.

'Or farm-hands,' she seethed, unable to leave it alone.

The car screeched to a halt outside her door and he spun to face her with terrifying speed.

'Or farm-hands,' he grated, 'however beautiful and willing.'

Before she could move he had her in his arms, fastening his fingers in her thick hair and taking her mouth by storm. He was angry, cruel and very determined, and for a minute her heart almost stopped. He was kissing her ruthlessly, shamelessly, allowing her no escape, forcing her head to his shoulder, his lips draining hers.

When his hand cupped her breast she trembled with shock, and, although he felt it, must have felt it, he never relented. His fingers found the tight nipple through the thin silken material, expertly bringing it to wild life, and when she moaned anxiously he lifted his head but his fingers still moved relentlessly.

'Isn't this what you expected?' he rasped, his eyes glittering down at her. 'An exciting end to an exciting evening? Surely this was considered when you and Celia planned your exquisite entrance? You were to lure me away from Auriel and protect Malcolm.'

She just shook her head numbly, unable to speak, and his fingers closed hard over her tender breast, possessive and ruthless.

'I'm glad you're not trying the lie in words, Georgina, because you've always been a poor liar. Did you plan it to the end? Am I supposed to take you to bed now?'

He seemed so menacing, not Steven at all, and she stared up at him with outright panic in her eyes, fighting down shameful excitement.

'Oh, please don't talk like that.' She was quite shocked out of anger. Her trembling fingers came up to close his lips but he pulled them away roughly, trapping them in one hard hand.

'I want to take you to bed,' he threatened harshly. 'Frustration is not at all easy to bear and I think an evening with you would wipe out plenty of my frustration.'

When she just stared at him, trembling all over, he opened the car door on to the cold night air and almost thrust her out. 'Go home, Georgina! If you weren't so damned tiny and beautiful I'd give you a good hiding! Next time you tempt me you might not get off so lightly!'

She just fled, and it was only as she stood shaking in her room that she realised she was quite ashamed of herself. And it was no use blaming Celia. She had been part of a great master plan that had gone hideously wrong. She sat in front of the dressing-table mirror and looked at herself as if she had never seen her own image before.

Steven had treated her with real contempt. She looked as if she had been thoroughly ravished and her breasts were still sharply pointed, tingling with excitement. She was scared too. Steven had almost said outright that he would take his frustrations out on her. He still wanted Auriel and he would have to face Auriel every day, knowing she was going to marry Malcolm.

What a terrible mess! She got ready for bed very quickly, putting out the light, and when her father came back much later and knocked she answered sleepily, although she was sure she would never sleep again.

'Are you all right, love?' he asked from the doorway.

'Just tired; goodnight.'

'That's a relief. Goodnight, love. I knew you must be all right or Steven would have stayed with you.'

She had to stuff her hand into her mouth to stop the hysteria until the door closed. Steven would have stayed with her! The way he was looking at her he could have killed her for not being Auriel. It made tears spring into her eyes and she couldn't stop them.

Even so, as she finally calmed down and drifted to sleep, his words lingered. He had said she was beautiful, even though he had said it angrily. She would keep up the image in future, even when she was working. Neat and petite. That would be her and there wasn't a thing Miss Auriel Delafield could do about that. *She* was about six feet tall, being a model. Both Steven and Malcolm must be quite mad. So was Celia. Maybe it ran in the family?

CHAPTER FOUR

CELIA had a very bad head the next day. Too much champagne, according to Sir Graham, who put Georgina through to Celia's room. This morning Georgina hadn't had the necessary nerve to simply go up to the hall. If Celia wanted to ride with her she would have to get herself round to the stables.

'I can't come,' Celia complained moodily. 'My head's killing me.'

'You're in the best place,' Georgina informed her tartly. 'If you get up Steven might kill you.'

'Was it as bad as all that? He looked furious when he came back.'

'Not as furious as he was earlier, believe me. In future count me out of your plans. He was on to us right from the word go and I don't suppose it did a bit of good.'

'None,' Celia moaned. 'When he came back he charmed Auriel right off her feet. That's why I've got a bad head—drowning my sorrows.'

'So there you are,' Georgina snapped, her heart sinking at the thought of Steven charming Auriel.

'And here I stay,' Celia muttered. 'He can't get me here.'

'Don't bank on it. If he wants you he'll get you.'

So she had her ride alone, giving Stardust some pretty vigorous exercise and ignoring her own bruised condition. It was nothing that a good hot bath wouldn't ease and she needed to free her mind of Steven at all costs.

She was unsaddling when Auriel marched up in the very latest riding gear, straight out of a glossy magazine and not exactly practical. Keeping up the neat petite image, Georgina had put on a white blouse beneath a deep blue sweater, her figure trim in riding trousers. She had even given her boots a good shine. Auriel looked down her lofty nose and eyed Stardust.

'Oh. Leave that saddled up. I'll take it out.'

'Sorry,' Georgina said quietly. 'This is my horse.'

'Well! I've never heard such cheek. Just because you've picked him out for yourself.'

'Her,' Georgina corrected. 'I didn't pick her out. I bought her and reared her. Stardust is mine—like personal property.'

'I'm surprised they let you keep it here. A horse eats a good deal.'

'Like a horse,' Georgina agreed wryly. 'I'm sure Joe will pick a horse out for you.'

'I can pick my own. I'll take that one,' Auriel announced crossly, looking at Royal, who sneered at her.

'No, you won't, miss,' Joe ordered, coming up quickly. 'That's a stallion and a handful for a man. He'd kill you. I reckon only Mr Steven could manage him.'

'Oh, he's so good at everything,' Auriel breathed, and the way she said it warned Georgina that Steven was near by. He was. He walked into the yard almost on cue, smiling at Auriel and then looking closely at Georgina's subdued face.

'Surely you're not going riding?'

'I've been,' Georgina murmured, avoiding his eyes and getting down to unsaddling. He looked a bit more forgiving this morning, but *she* wasn't forgiving him and he wasn't going to use her to make Auriel jealous either.

'Ignoring the bruises?'

'They'll improve.' She shrugged and turned away. She didn't want to speak to him and she didn't want to see him with Auriel. He looked as if he was about to say more, but Auriel was standing there all a-glitter and Joe came up anyway.

'This lady wanted to ride Royal, Mr Steven. I took it upon myself to refuse. I imagine you'll want to take him out.'

'I imagine I won't have much choice,' Steven said wryly. 'Saddle him up, Joe.'

'Even that's dangerous enough,' Joe muttered, but he went off to obey. Steven took the saddle out of Georgina's hands but he didn't speak to her.

'Joe will get you a horse,' he said, smiling at Auriel, and of course she had to try.

'I fancied that one.' She nodded at Stardust and Georgina clenched her fists to keep her temper. Much more of this and the balloon would go up!

'She's Georgina's, aren't you, my beauty?' He ran his hand over Stardust, who shivered in delight. 'So is this saddle,' he added, carting it into the tack-room. Auriel flashed Georgina a look of pure hatred, but she had certainly got the message. Here one did not take other people's possessions. Georgina hoped Steven would remember that when he rode off with Auriel. She knew perfectly well why he had unsaddled for her and carried it away. He was playing on Auriel's feelings, making her want to go back to him.

'Can I ride with you, Steven?' Auriel gushed as Joe led Royal out.

'I think not,' he murmured, not really paying attention, his eyes on the black stallion, who looked all set for mischief. 'I think today the ride is going to be hard work.'

'Just watch him!' Joe said a bit anxiously.

'He's making a damned good job of watching me,' Steven remarked, swinging into the saddle.

Royal balked at once, throwing up his head, rolling his eyes and doing his best to unseat Steven, who sat tall and determined, pitting his will against the great horse.

'The devil!' Joe breathed worriedly, and Georgina found that her nails were clenched into her palms as Royal paced angrily round the yard, shaking his head, determined to be master.

Suddenly Steven wheeled him hard and put him straight at the high fence, which he took like a bird, flying over.

'Oh, what a dangerous thing to do!' Auriel breathed.

'T'weren't. That horse has got to know who's boss. Now he knows. Though nobody else would have had the nerve,' Joe said with admiration.

They watched Steven put Royal through his paces in the near paddock, and then he trotted back into the yard, patting the strong neck, Royal looking slightly puzzled. Steven merely looked amused.

'Now we'll go for a ride,' he announced. 'This horse is under-exercised, Joe.'

'Are you surprised?' Joe asked drily.

Steven looked down at Georgina. From his position on the great black horse he made her feel minute, insignificant.

'Disappointed?' he queried softly.

'I never expected he could throw you.' She looked up at him firmly and he raised one supercilious eyebrow.

'I can see that,' he murmured drily and it was only then that she realised she was still clutching Joe's arm. She turned away impatiently and heard Steven's low laugh; then he was talking to Auriel in a quiet murmur.

'Meet me down by the end of the home woods in about twenty minutes. I'll show you around the estate.'

Auriel smiled knowingly and Georgina knew she had been expecting it. They had worked it out beforehand, no doubt. She walked off, biting at her lip in annoyance.

It was Malcolm's job to show his fiancée around. He should have been out riding with her too. What was he going to do? Wait until Steven took her away from him? How did they have the nerve? Right under Malcolm's nose. At any time he might come out and see them, and then he would see the full picture, just as she had.

She glanced round, but Steven was already galloping down the hill, his black hair gleaming in the morning sunlight. He wasn't wearing a hard hat. He never expected to be thrown. It hadn't happened in living memory. She turned away, glaring. At that moment she felt like making a clay image and sticking pins in it, but she wasn't sure who it would turn out to be, Steven or Auriel.

In spite of her father's remonstrations about riding and doubts about work, she worked. Something had to take her mind off what Steven and Auriel were doing. She hadn't realised she was capable of so many lurid thoughts. An hour later she was driving the Land Rover across the fields from the Home Farm when she saw Steven riding out from the woods.

For a minute her mind could only see how truly magnificent he looked, the great black horse pacing along strongly, Steven with his dark head thrown back in that arrogant way. The devil and friend, she thought sourly. And what had he done with Auriel? Was she still lurking about in the woods? It was dark and private in there. Anything could happen. She drove off angrily but as she got out to open the gate into the lane Steven suddenly confronted her, sitting the horse as if he were part of it, looking down at her imperiously.

'How did you get here?' She was angry with him, so angry, knowing perfectly well he had just left Auriel.

'I still know all the short cuts. I saw you watching me.'

'I was not watching you! I was admiring Royal. Your father made a good buy there. When we breed from him it's——'

'We?' he queried superciliously, looking down his haughty nose at her.

'I'm part of the establishment, like it or not. I'm an estate worker, according to Miss Delafield.'

'Got under your tough little hide, has she?'

'Not at all,' Georgina murmured loftily. 'I *am* an estate worker. It's what I'll always do.'

'Only until your father retires,' he said, suddenly cold. 'When he does I'll need a new manager.'

'Please God, you won't have inherited!'

'I don't need to. Haven't you heard, George? I'm taking over completely.' For a second she almost shrank away, every black thought come to fruition.

'You can't be serious! Your father would never——'

'Running Templeton Estates is damned hard work. We're big business and getting bigger.' He looked down at her coolly. 'People retire. My father is tired. When Harry retires I'll have to look very carefully for another manager.'

'What's wrong with me? I'm qualified.'

'Qualified to be a thorn in the flesh. There are quite a few men on the other estates who are ready for promotion. I'm not likely to pass them over for you. In any case, you'll be long gone; surely you're marrying Jeremy?'

'I haven't decided,' she said with dignity. She wished Jeremy were here now to soothe her and tell Steven that she wouldn't need to work if she didn't want to.

'Now *that's* sound sense. I wasn't sure if you had any.' He tightened the reins and prepared to move off, still throwing his barbs. 'The trouble is, George, I don't think Mrs Ripley will let Jeremy marry until he's grown up.'

'I've told you, he's twenty-five!' Georgina stormed, forgetting dignity altogether. The hell with dignity. Steven infuriated her.

'But young with it,' he mused. 'Consider the poor woman. With you married to dear Jeremy she would have two children to take care of instead of one.'

'Jeremy doesn't need taking care of and neither do I!' she said hotly, glaring up at him.

He simply wheeled Royal away.

'You always did,' he reminded her softly. '*I* took care of you.'

He put the horse into a canter and she stared after him with tears of rage in her eyes. He looked so damned magnificent and he was hateful, hateful!

'I—hate—you!' She shouted it at the top of her voice and she didn't care either if anyone else heard. He never even turned. He simply raised one acknowledging hand and then he was gone. She got back in the Land Rover and had a little cry of rage. He was going to take everything away from her, cut her off from all her happiness. He was going to get Auriel, too, because who could resist Steven? Well, if he married Auriel she wouldn't want to be here anyway. Maybe it was all for the best.

In spite of the bleak outlook, over the next week she maintained the planned image. A visit to the hairdresser's proved to be a great success and the plait was banished for good, her hair now simply shoulder-length, its natural wave restored. Celia went with her on a shopping spree at the weekend and, contrary to her expectations, she enjoyed it and came back feeling feminine and rather smug.

Jeremy wasn't too sure. He told her he liked her as she had been. He also told her she was too beautiful to need to change her image, and it gave a great boost to her morale. She was accepting every invitation at the moment, going out with him far more regularly than before. He was a steadying influence if nothing else, and she had to admit he was very good to her. She was comfortable with Jeremy. She never felt either the need to fight him or the need to fall at his feet.

Steven had gone to London for a few days—trouble with one of their firms there—and Auriel had jumped at the chance to go with him.

'Oh, good! You can give me a lift down, Steven. My agent rang today—a really fabulous job.'

Malcolm showed anger, real anger, for the first time ever.

'I thought we had agreed that now you're engaged the jobs would finish?'

'But, darling, we're not married yet. I could use the cash and, in any case, I miss London.'

'Then I'll take you down.'

'Nonsense. You're needed here. I'll whiz down with Steven.'

Georgina was keeping well clear of the hall and of Steven, but all this was relayed by Celia, word for word.

'Of course, she won,' Celia muttered. 'One thing, though: Malcolm has noticed at last. He was looking furious as they drove off.'

'How was Steven looking?' Georgina asked carefully, hating herself for the interest.

'Amused. I don't know what's got into Steven.'

Georgina did. Auriel was his property that Malcolm had inadvertently taken. She couldn't understand why Celia didn't see it. Nobody ever questioned Steven. He was a law unto himself. In London he could do anything. He would be living at his flat with Auriel. The thought twisted her up inside.

Mrs Ripley wasn't too sure of Georgina's new image either. Each time they went out Jeremy picked up Georgina and then just had to 'nip back' to see if his mother was all right. Since she had become a widow Jeremy was very protective of her and in a way it was charming, although Georgina always felt slightly uncomfortable with his mother.

'That's the third new outfit in two weeks, Georgina,' Mrs Ripley said with an edge of disapproval. 'It's not very practical, is it?'

'Just depends what you're doing,' Georgina said breezily. 'This is fine for the Farmers' Club dance.'

'The others won't be in silk,' Mrs Ripley pointed out sternly, crossing her arms and running her eyes over Georgina's brown silk skirt and matching top.

'Poor them. They should spend their money.'

Georgina was beginning to get a bit rattled, and Jeremy was determined not to take sides.

'They have more important things to spend money on,' Mrs Ripley said with open disapproval now.

Like wellington boots? Georgina picked up her bag and pointedly moved to the door.

'There's no need for me to save up. Anyway, I'll be getting married, I expect.' She just threw it in to see what would happen, and Mrs Ripley gasped. Jeremy flushed but his eyes lit up.

'Not *now*, though,' he laughed, reassuring his mother.

'I should think not! Far too young.'

Who was? Georgina mused about it all the way to the dance and right through the evening. Would she always be too young? Steven had told her she was too young at eighteen, and clearly Jeremy and his mother thought her too young now. How old did you have to be?

Jeremy kissed her goodnight with just a touch more ardour, but she didn't go spinning away like a leaf. There was no inclination to go into a sensual daze. She tried to like it but Steven's face kept coming into her mind and she was nearly in tears.

What was the point of changing her image anyway? Jeremy had always liked her as she was; she wasn't interested in flirting with anyone else. The fact of the matter was, Steven had said she was beautiful. A lot of good that did her. He was a traitor, a philanderer, a phantom from the dead past. She brooded on it for a whole week, and when Steven came back she avoided Kellerdale Hall all over again. If he noticed he did nothing about it. She never even saw him. Auriel had stayed down in London and Malcolm, according to Celia, was like a bear with a sore head. Georgina wondered if he also knew deep down that Auriel and Steven had been together down there.

A week later Georgina had a rather terrible confrontation. It happened without warning but somehow, unexpected as it was, it was a catalyst and changed everything completely with no going back.

She was right on the edge of the estate, fairly close to the main road, and she turned into the lane home as it was getting well into the afternoon. It was a fairly dismal day. It had been raining and for once she had let her image slip a little. In jeans and thick green jacket, her hair a little wet and a lot wild, she closed the gate and went back to the Land Rover to find herself facing a complete stranger.

The sight of him, here on the estate on a dark afternoon, had her stopping at once, her senses attuned to danger. It wasn't that he was a particularly big man but there was something about him that worried her. He was good-looking in a way, dark brown hair and dark eyes, and he was certainly well-dressed, but the look in his eyes was disturbing. He was watching her intently, his eyes gleaming. As she knew she looked a mess it put her on to instant alert.

'Good. A maiden to the rescue. I seem to have lost my way.' He was smiling, but that was easy enough for anyone and Georgina certainly didn't smile back.

As far as she could see, he was on foot. A man like that, tramping about wet countryside? Her suspicions grew and she edged her way to the Land Rover.

'Where do you want to be?' she asked casually, trying to look taller.

'Well, the hall, of course.'

'What hall?' Anybody could say that. It wasn't long ago that a girl had been attacked not too far away. She weighed up her chances of making a dive for the Land Rover and gave up the idea at once. She would never be able to get the doors locked in time. It was all up to her instincts of self-preservation.

There was a big broken stick by the hedge and she ran her hand over it casually, testing its weight. It would do at a pinch.

'Er—why? Kellerdale Hall.' He was looking at her more closely than ever and he took a step nearer.

'Where's your car?' Georgina rapped out, her hand closing over the stick.

'Down there.' He waved his hand further down the lane but the hedges were high and Georgina wasn't taking her eyes off him. Anybody could say that too. It seemed to her that he was edging closer, and the skin on her arms chilled with apprehension.

He looked a bit exasperated when all she did was stare at him, and he took his hands out of his pockets.

'Look, darling. Try to be a bit more co-operative.' He seemed to move quickly then and Georgina panicked. She wasn't about to co-operate with what he had in mind. She lashed out with the stick, and although she was petite she was no weakling. It caught him at the side of the head and he went down like a log.

Things seemed to happen with bewildering speed. As the man went down there was a roar of sound and Steven's Porsche tore in from the road end. He was just in time to see the main event and it was all too much for Georgina's pent-up nerves. She screamed.

'What the hell do you think you're doing?'

Steven grabbed her and removed the stick, giving her a shake, keeping hold of her as he glanced at the man who was now struggling upwards.

'Are you OK, Arnold?'

'God knows.' He shook his dazed head and Steven turned back to his captive, his black frown firmly fixed.

'Explain yourself!' He looked much more threatening than the man had ever looked, and now she could see her position more clearly. It was bad.

'I—I thought he was going to attack me.'

'*Thought?*' Steven glared at her. 'So you got your retaliation in first? My God. You always were a lunatic.'

He let her go and she just fell against the side of the Land Rover, very shaken, in more ways than one, and rather ashamed of herself for panicking.

'What's the damage, Arnold?' He went across and helped the man to stand completely upright.

'Oh, I expect I'll survive. It wasn't so much the blow, you understand, as the unexpected attack, wet path and so on, although she packs a hefty swing for a dainty doll. I'm glad you know her.' He glanced warily at Georgina and she gave him a weak smile that didn't seem to reassure him at all. He didn't smile back and looked heartily relieved that Steven was there.

Steven suddenly laughed, the tension easing from him.

'Don't let it put you off that you met the local madwoman first. Normally we have her under control.' He paused to introduce them. 'Georgina, this is Arnold Lang, my right-hand man. Just get a close look at him. I don't want you to go for him again, understand?'

She didn't think it was so funny anyway. She was so shaken that she couldn't yet get into the driving seat. She wondered if he would have thought it so funny if she had simply given up and let herself be attacked. It was all right for Steven. *She* wasn't a blue-eyed giant!

'Where's your car?' Steven asked.

'Down there. I told her,' Arnold said with a reproachful look at Georgina.

'She's trained to attack strangers,' Steven murmured with altogether uncalled-for sarcasm. 'Think you can make it? It's straight down the lane now. You can't miss the hall.'

'I can make it. The surprise is passing off. And that's all you needed to say,' he added, looking at Georgina. 'Straight down the lane. It would have saved a lot of trouble.'

'I'm really very sorry,' Georgina managed shakily. 'But you were looking at me.' She could see that confirmed her insanity.

'I don't normally close my eyes when I see a beautiful girl. If it's a local rule, though, I'll do it in future. You don't get to hear about these things in London.'

He went off and Steven turned back to her.

'Now you, Miss Summers,' he said with a return to grimness.

'I'm sorry. I'll go home.' She moved on shaky legs but he was close to her instantly.

'You're still shaking. Little idiot.' He pulled her close and she was so churned up that she just let him. 'He really frightened you, didn't he?'

She nodded her head, looking down at her wet boots.

'He sort of just appeared and I couldn't see any car. It's a bit isolated out here.'

'It is,' Steven said grimly. 'I think it's about time you stopped this estate-managing business, Georgina.'

'Oh! Don't send me away!' She looked up at him with pleading eyes, still trembling and on the very edge of tears.

'Would it be so very bad?' He gazed down at her and she was so prepared to beg that she just looked back at him helplessly.

'I don't think I could even live. Everything—everything here is my life.' Tears swam in her eyes. He watched her for a minute and then turned her away.

'I'll drive you back. I'll send a couple of the boys down to pick up the Land Rover.'

He had the hood up now on the car, protecting them from the rain, and it was warm and cosy but she gave a little shiver.

'You know, I thought he was going to kiss me.' She was speaking to him as she had always spoken to him long ago, momentarily forgetting Auriel, his crimes and everything else.

'Maybe he even thought about it. You've got a wild and beautiful look about you today.' She had to ignore that because right now she couldn't cope with it.

'Anyway,' she finished, 'that's why I hit him.'

'Because you don't like being kissed. Surely Jeremy kisses you? I hear you've been going out with him almost nightly since I came back.'

'We're very good friends.' She hung her head, feeling the colour come back to her skin with a rush. He had to tease away at her even when she had been so shocked. Actually she knew she was going to cry and she wanted to get home first.

'I see. Jeremy kisses your hand,' he taunted. 'That's nice. I expect he read it in a book—*Boy's Annual*?'

He reached forward to the ignition and she was so pent up, so miserable, that she lashed out at him. His cruelty and sarcasm were just too much for her.

Of course, he was too quick. He caught her hand in mid-flight and held it fast.

'I don't keep still and let myself be beaten, Georgina. I'm not Arnold and I wasn't even thinking of kissing you.'

'You're a brute!' Suddenly tears spilled over on to her cheeks and she didn't even care if he knew.

'Why am I a brute? I just didn't *know* you wanted me to kiss you.'

'I don't!' She snatched her hand away and began frantically to wipe at her tears, but he leaned across and simply collected her, pulling her into his arms and looking down at her.

'You do,' he said quietly. 'You want me to hold you, to kiss you, to love you. Don't you, Georgina?'

And the trouble was, she did. Inside she admitted it, even though she shook her head wildly, the tears still streaming away on to her cheeks. She knew him, his treachery, his ways, his plans to get rid of her, his plans to get Auriel back for himself, but it didn't seem to matter sometimes.

She gave a wild little sob and he bent his night-black head, catching her mouth fiercely, and this time she didn't resist at all. Her lips opened under his and the kiss deepened and deepened. It was Steven. Steven. He was still beautiful to her, still the only one who could bring her blood to fire.

She was spinning again, falling and spinning wildly, and his fingers wiped her cheeks with hardly a pause in the kiss. She could hear her own frantic little cries but they only seemed to make him pull her closer. Her head was in the circle of his arm, her bright hair spilling over his sleeve, and she shivered as his hand found the zip of her jacket and pulled it down.

It was all some erotic dream she had dreamed at eighteen, maybe even at sixteen. The darkened car, the warmth and Steven's hands on her.

'Let me go.' A shred of sanity urged her to say it but she didn't mean it at all and he knew that too.

'I don't think I can. Not yet.' His breath was warm against her lips and when his hand slid beneath her sweater and found her breast, touching her skin for the first time ever, she just sank into him, her heart beating like the fluttering wings of a bird. She twisted closer and he lifted her higher into his arms, cradling her.

'Beautiful, wild Georgina,' he murmured thickly. 'Can you hear me or have you already gone off into that dreamy trance?'

She couldn't answer because she was too far away from reality, clinging to his lips with a sweetness that drove him further still. His hand stroked her breast until it was heavy and silken beneath his fingers and the whole world became distant, only the tang of his skin, the movement of his lips and hands real. Desire raged through her, sweet and painful, making her completely pliant until she was crushed against him, her mouth fused with his.

'Stop, Georgina!' His voice was suddenly taut, harsh, and he held her away as she looked at him with shimmering, dazed eyes. He straightened her sweater and gave her a gentle shake, and she knew he didn't want her at all. It was just that she had happened to be there. Maybe he was like that with all women. What did she know of him anyway?

Suddenly it was all over as it had always been all over. Tears filled her eyes, turning the honey to glittering amber, and he caught her face between two strong hands.

'Don't!' he ordered roughly. 'If you cry again I won't let you go. There's a limit to my ability to discipline myself when you catch fire in my arms. If this continues you won't be alone in that little trance. You'll have your first lover. This is neither the time nor the place, however much it hurts to stop.'

Right now she was too lost to feel shame, but she knew perfectly well that the shame would come. Steven was experienced, older, and maybe some responsibility from the past stayed him. Certainly she hadn't protested. Certainly she had just fallen into his arms, letting him touch her, kiss her.

'I'm sorry.' Her voice was trembling, her hands shaking, and he sighed, moving away from her and starting the car.

'So am I, Georgina, because you don't trust me one inch, do you? All that went a long time ago, out through the door with your childhood.'

'You still treat me like a child, a mad child,' she choked, and he gave a hard laugh.

'Think again, Sunflower. Seconds ago I was stroking your breast. I acknowledge your womanhood. The trouble is, I despise your suspicion.'

But what did he expect? There was Auriel for sure. And Malcolm? What about poor, kind Malcolm? Finally Steven would get rid of her, turn her away from her beloved Kellerdale Hall, from the woods and fields she had roamed since childhood.

She would never want anyone else to touch her ever again in her life, not after Steven. It was one more thing. She closed her eyes and said nothing, and when he stopped at the Dower House she just walked off without looking back, bursting into tears when she heard the car move smoothly away. There was a time when he would not have simply gone. He would have come in and held her, cradled her against him and called her George until she was better and angry and normal. As far as she could see, he had ruined her life and meant to go on doing it until she was gone for good.

CHAPTER FIVE

THERE was a lifetime arrangement of dinner at the hall on the last Friday of the month. Normally Georgina looked forward to it. Her father and Sir Graham disappeared into the study and she settled down to talk to Lady Evelyn and later to have a good gossip with Celia. This time, of course, it was different.

She wasn't avoiding Steven, he was ignoring her, and Auriel had returned. Malcolm had become aloof, behaving quite curtly to Auriel, according to Celia, and Arnold Lang was back again—good news for Celia, who liked him, but a bit embarrassing for Georgina, who had flattened him.

Nothing, of course, would ever be the same again, she mused as she got ready. As far as she could see, her own position was untenable. She couldn't get out of anything without hurting the people she loved. Her whole life here had been one of ease and happiness as far as her relations with the Templetons was concerned and her father would never understand even if she could tell him. As to Lady Evelyn, she would be horrified. She couldn't even tell Celia.

She swung round to look at herself. Nowadays she seemed to look much older, and unless she was mistaken she was losing what bit of weight she had. Mrs Ripley said she was getting skinny and eyed her suspiciously as if there were some deep plan behind it. As it was she was just uneasy and unhappy.

It gave her a sort of ethereal look though that went well with the sea-green chiffon dress she wore, another new buy. Once it had started she couldn't seem to stop this shopping business. It took her mind off things for a while, but everything came back when she was alone.

She clipped on her earrings and went down to join her father, who was already waiting.

'You get more beautiful,' he said with a fond smile. 'A few weeks ago you were still a tomboy. Now you're a woman. One day you're going to be swept off your feet.'

'I'm set on being an old maid,' she pointed out, laughing up at him.

'Being set won't do a lot of good when some man decides he's ready to get married.'

'Mrs Ripley says we're too young.'

'That woman! Good grief. Who said anything about young Ripley anyway? I hope he's not a serious contender. I doubt if I could swallow that.'

'I like Jeremy,' she said seriously. 'He's very good to me, you know. He hasn't asked me but I really think he wants to marry me one day.'

'It sounds businesslike.' Her father touched her cheek fondly. 'Is that what you want? A nice, safe marriage?'

'Jeremy fits into our world,' she murmured, not knowing her eyes were wistful.

'Does he, love? Your world has always been the Templetons.'

'It can't go on being like that,' Georgina pointed out, moving fretfully away. 'When you retire I expect we'll leave all this. We're not really part of their world.'

'They've taken damned good care to keep you in it,' her father said flatly. 'They've loved you since you were a child.'

'I know.' Georgina sat on the arm of a chair and twisted her hands anxiously. 'I adore Lady Evelyn and Sir Graham. Celia has always been my best friend and— and Malcolm...'

'Aren't we going to mention Steven?'

She hung her head, her skin flushing painfully.

'Oh, Steven!' She managed an offhand little laugh. 'He thinks I'm mad.'

Harry Summers's face softened as he looked down at her, his smile hidden for a minute. 'Well, of course sparks tend to fly when you two meet,' he pointed out. 'I don't expect he realises you've grown up.'

She nearly laughed and gave the game away. Not realise she was grown up? Hadn't he kissed her, held her, threatened to be her first lover? He knew she was grown up all right and she was also a very good cover for his renewed affair with Auriel—if she was stupid enough.

'Anyway,' her father continued, seeing the wild emotion that raced across her expressive face and deciding to keep out of things, 'whoever marries young Ripley is stuck with a mother-in-law and a half—think on that. And I'll tell you this, that woman will live forever. She's determined on it.'

They were still laughing as they went into the hall and Georgina was glad. She knew the smile would be wiped off her face as soon as she saw Steven.

'Is it all right to stare now?' Arnold Lang came up and smiled at Georgina, Celia grinning beside him. Of course, they had all heard the tale, although Georgina had been assured that it had not come from Steven. It broke the ice.

'I'm still embarrassed,' Georgina said with a wry look.

'You can certainly take care of yourself,' Arnold mused, rubbing his head reminiscently.

'Not according to Steven,' Celia piped up, much too loudly. 'Steven has taken care of her since she was an infant. Given half a chance he'd still do it.'

Georgina glared at her and then went quite pale as Steven walked up. He just didn't look at her at all; he never did nowadays.

'Ready, Harry? We'll get half an hour in before dinner. You'd better come along, Arnold—that's what you're here for, even if Celia thinks you're here to entertain her.' He turned on his heel and the men followed, Malcolm too being swept up *en route*. This was all new. So Steven was taking over. The easy-going old times would end. Sir Graham looked greatly relieved, but to Georgina it was like the crack of doom.

'I take it that you two are not speaking?' Celia put in as the others left. She was still a little pink in the face after Steven's remark, and Georgina couldn't help thinking it served her right. She was sure that Steven had heard his sister's words and it had only added to her own misery. If she fell in a deep pit now Steven would merely look over the edge with total uninterest.

'We have nothing to say to each other,' Georgina snapped.

'Don't take it out on me. I mean, I can't understand it. I always thought Steven adored you, and look at you now: a dream, ready to be swept off your feet.'

'I'm grown up, Celia, no longer a child for Steven to protect. I was grateful while it lasted but it was a long time ago. Let it drop, please—completely.' Celia must have seen something in her face because she tucked her arm into Georgina's and led her off, skilfully changing direction when she saw Auriel.

Auriel could not be avoided at dinner, though. Georgina found herself seated opposite Steven and the little appetite she had nowadays vanished. She was grateful for Arnold's amused interest in her and grateful to Celia, who became very protective and frequently leaned across Arnold to speak to her.

'Isn't this a wonderful old place?' Auriel announced, looking with a sort of proprietorial air around the huge old dining-room. 'Did you know that the Templetons came over with the Norman Conquest?' she asked Arnold.

'Er—yes, I did, actually.' His speed of reply didn't get him off the hook. It was no use telling the family, who knew, and she scorned even to speak to Georgina and her father, so Arnold had to hear.

'The first one was Sir John Templeton,' she recounted. 'The first one with an English sort of name. He had three sons but two of them died...'

'One being hanged for murder,' Malcolm put in as if he was contemplating it. 'Do you think we could do without the history, Auriel?'

'Well, I'm so proud of myself for looking it up, darling. Maybe your farm bailiff and his daughter don't know.' There was a little shocked silence but not for long.

'Harry is more knowledgeable about things than any of us,' Sir Graham barked disapprovingly. 'He's the estate manager—not only of this estate either. Georgina is equally qualified.'

Georgina had never heard him so stroppy in her life, and her qualifications weren't going to do her a bit of good. Steven was going to get rid of her.

'Oh, I'm sorry. I'm sure I've said the wrong thing,' Auriel gurgled, quite unrepentant, looking innocently surprised that Celia and Sir Graham were both glaring at her. Arnold was looking a bit stunned. 'I just wanted to air my new knowledge,' she continued. 'You see, my family came over with the Normans too.'

'I expect the French couldn't off-load them quick enough,' Celia murmured, manners forgotten at this insult to Harry and Georgina.

'That will do, Celia!' Steven's voice just cracked across the table and Celia stared at him defiantly until her nerve broke.

There had never been a dinner like this before. All the tranquillity of the old hall was shattered. After dinner the men went off again but this time Malcolm and Arnold seemed to have been excused and, as Celia was clearly interested in their new guest and Steven was unavailable, Auriel had to content herself with Malcolm, who didn't look as if he could be coaxed at this moment.

Georgina wandered out on to the terrace, braving the quite cold air. She looked out over the moonlit estate, loving it, grieving for the time they would have to leave it. It had not escaped her attention that Steven had snapped out when Celia had had a dig at Auriel. Sir Graham had been the one to defend her and her father, not that he had been slow off the mark. Steven wouldn't have bothered, though, not now. There wasn't much doubt that he was involved with Auriel.

Steven suddenly appeared behind her and she stiffened instantly. Having just been running his crimes through her mind, she was prepared to defend herself.

'Surely you're cold out here?'

'Only a little. I'm taking a last look at all this. I doubt if I'll come to dinner again, and of course now that you've taken over it's only a matter of time before I have to leave the estate, isn't it?'

'Georgina!' He stepped close but she backed away rapidly, hating him and loving him all at the same time.

'Don't try any of your Norman Conquests on me! Just content yourself with Auriel's adulation until you can get back down to London with her.'

It stopped him dead in his tracks. His eyes were a cold glitter in the moonlight.

'Auriel is engaged to my brother.'

'I'm almost engaged to Jeremy but it didn't stop you kissing me. I don't suppose it stops you with her either, especially as she throws herself at you. Did she turn to Malcolm because you weren't faithful, or did she make a mistake and think he was the one who would be boss here when your father dies?'

Even in the moonlight she could see he was white with rage. She knew she had gone too far also, blurting out all her anguished thoughts. He made a slight movement towards her, utterly menacing, and she took to her heels like a terrified deer, racing down the steps and across the moonlit lawn, her dress flowing out behind her, shimmering in the moonlight.

He would kill her, he surely would, and nobody would be able to save her. There was violence in Steven tonight. Probably there had always been violence there but she just hadn't noticed before. She hadn't made it to the trees when he caught her, sweeping her up and striding into the summer-house, slamming the door and then just letting her drop.

How she kept her feet she didn't know, and she backed away from him, grateful for the moonlight that flooded the room and gave her some idea of where he was. Steven in a rage was no person to encounter and she had brought it all on herself. It was no use pleading now. She could see it all—'Death in the Summer-house'.

'So I'm the worst kind of villain,' he said coldly. 'I steal my brother's fiancée, having first discarded her. I throw poor defenceless females out into the cruel world.'

'I'm not defenceless,' she managed through shaking lips.

'No, by God, you're not. You've got a tongue like a sharp knife and you don't much care where it strikes. I think I'd rather have the blunt instrument like Arnold.'

'Why do you have to be the way you are?' she suddenly cried pitifully, grieving for her lost Steven, wanting him back so much that it hurt all over.

'How am I, Georgina? It seems I'm your great enemy. I used to be your friend; more than your friend.'

'I didn't know then how treacherous you could be.'

'Treacherous?' He was back to dangerous, menacing anger, but she couldn't stop.

'Yes, treacherous. I find out more every day.'

'I used to think you were nice, sweet, and normal. I never knew quite how crazy you were,' he snapped caustically. He pounced on her suddenly, pulling her savagely into his arms. 'Don't panic,' he rasped. 'I'm all set to cure you. Maybe I should prove I'm exactly what you think. That being the case, there'll be no need for me to stop this time, will there?'

She gave a muffled cry but his mouth crushed it, his hands holding her with scornful ease when she struggled.

'You ran off into the night, Georgina,' he taunted against her mouth, tightening his grip. 'I don't expect they'll search for you yet. There's plenty of time.'

He really meant it. He was crushing her, ravaging her soft lips, bending her over his arm until she thought her neck would break.

She began to tremble violently, soft murmurs of panic breathed against his lips, and as suddenly as it had come his temper eased, his arms now just an iron-strong shelter.

'You crazy little wild cat. You're jealous,' he murmured, scattering caresses all over her face.

'I'm not! I'm not!'

'Of course you are. You always were—jealous, possessive, passionate. Do you think I never saw those golden eyes watching me? I could have taken you when you were sixteen. You wanted me then.'

'Oh, you're wicked, so wicked. I never really knew you, did I?'

'You will, Sunflower, completely.'

He had finished talking and all she knew was that she was drifting back into the strange little world she inhabited when he kissed her. She was falling and his arms were holding her up, his lips moving over hers, his hands stroking her back through the wispy material of her gown. She loved him; it came down to that, but he must never know. Even if he took her now, and she could never make a move to stop him, she would never confess how she felt. Some part of her would always be secret, safe from Steven. It was the only safety she had.

'Georgina!' His lips trailed like fire over her neck, his hands tightly possessive on her hips, and she knew it would not be long before his own hold on sanity fled. They were safe in the darkness, more alone with each other than they had ever seemed to be before.

Rescue came from an unexpected quarter. Auriel was walking from the house, shouting for Steven, her voice like a carefully coached nightingale, and it brought Georgina back to earth with a bang. Even while he was holding her, caressing her, that woman was looking for him as if she had every right to do so, which she almost certainly had.

Steven stiffened angrily but Georgina took the opportunity to pull out of his arms and back away on shaking legs.

'Better hurry before she screams with frustration. I'll just hide here and she'll never know how badly you've let her down.'

For a second he stared at her angrily and then smiled a very cold smile for all his recent passion.

'So you've really declared war on me, Georgina? All right. I take up any challenge. Let me know when you've pulled down the flag.'

'Never in my whole life,' she spat.

'Never is a long time. And, Georgina, I'm home for good.'

'For bad, really for bad. Listen to her getting agitated. Between you you'll break Mal's heart.'

'I intend to break yours first, Georgina. After that I'll get around to other people. Don't forget that I have all the advantages. You want me. I intend to get you.'

He just walked out and left her, joining Auriel on the moonlit lawn, and Georgina peered through the window, watching them until they were back in the house. Her fists clenched and temper flushed out the remaining wisps of dreamy enchantment. He thought he could have everything, reach for her when he felt like it, take Malcolm's hateful fiancée, go down to London with her to some—some love-nest! Yes, she had declared war! She would show him just how much.

As a matter of priority she had her motorbike repaired. Since the accident Steven had not mentioned it once, being accustomed to obedience. Now, however, defiance had set in in a big way and everything he said would be scorned. After all, what could he do? He was already going to get rid of her. Nothing could be worse than that.

All the same, she was glad it was safely out of sight when he came down to the Dower House in the morning a week later.

'Where's Harry?' He started right in with no pleasant preliminaries, his face like granite.

'He's over at Little Ripton. Can I help?' She was coolly polite, very pleased with her attitude. If he could play the master she could play the obedient serf.

'These reports are wrong.' He tossed a sheaf of papers on the table. 'Let him know when he comes back.'

She glanced at the papers and then her head shot up angrily.

'They can't be wrong. I did them.'

'Then you'll be able to find the mistakes, won't you? It doesn't add up correctly. Thank heavens it wasn't Harry. I thought he must be slipping.'

'Oh, I'll never be able to fill his shoes. I know that,' she seethed, cool deference forgotten.

'In no way at all. You'll not get the chance. I think we've established that,' he stated coldly. It made tears sting at the back of her eyes and she snatched the papers up, glaring at them.

'I'm sure you'll find the mistake with a couple of hours' work. While we're on the subject of work, there are two broken gates at the road end of the estate. See to it.'

He turned to leave and she yelled at him.

'I can't be everywhere at once!'

'You ride with Celia every morning. As far as I can see, that's pleasure. Work seems to begin for you at about ten. Every other worker on the estate starts at eight.'

'So now I'm a worker on the estate?' she raged. 'I'm to be part of a time and motion study?'

'It won't be necessary. Put in the time and I'm sure the motion will take care of itself. As to being a worker on the estate, you've assured me that you are that and only that with boring regularity. The function of a worker is to work. See to those two gates.'

He walked off, slamming the door, and it put her into such a fury that she threw her lunch away and got straight into the Land Rover to go round for the estate joiner, who left his lunch too when he heard about Mr Steven's annoyance. And Georgina toured the estate with eyes like an eagle, looking for any signs of neglect. When Jeremy rang that night she snapped his head off and had to apologise. Then she spent two hours going through the papers to find a tiny little mistake that Steven could have pointed out to her in a second. Her fury was still at full boil when she went to bed.

She was out at half-past seven the next morning and up at the stables, saddling Stardust and leading her out, and her face mirrored her rage when Steven came into the yard looking like a hero in a white polo-necked sweater and jeans.

'Riding?' he asked threateningly, quite used to her defiance.

'No.' She glanced at her watch. 'It's seven-forty, Mr Steven. At the moment I'm on my own time. I'll be out with my pitchfork with the other lads at eight.'

'Listen, you pint-sized witch...!' He took a step towards her but she met his blazing blue gaze with wide honey-coloured bewilderment.

'I'm only following orders, sir.' She thought he was going to explode with fury, but Celia appeared at the critical moment.

'What goes on?' Her eyes flashed from one to the other. 'Riding without me, Gina? That strikes me as mean.'

'I shall not be riding from now on,' Georgina stated firmly. 'I'm moving my horse to other quarters and, if you'll excuse me, it's getting late. I have to start work at eight.'

'What's the matter with you?' Celia grabbed her arm. 'Stardust has always been here. That's her place.'

'There's a small loose-box behind the Dower House. I'll keep her there in future. The stables are for the family. I'm ashamed I never realised it before.' Her small, quiet dignity quite shocked Celia, and clearly infuriated Steven to the edge of murder.

'What have you been saying to her?' Celia snapped, rounding on her brother for the first time in her life.

'Keep out of this!' he warned through gritted teeth.

'I will not! Gina is my friend.'

'Then heaven help you,' he growled. 'I hope you can cope with her.' He strode off, evidently discarding whatever he had come to do, and Celia stared after him worriedly.

'What's got into him? He's quite nasty.'

'Hah!' Georgina muttered in triumph, leading Stardust out. 'Now you find out. I'll tell you one final thing: I'm not allowed to ride with you any more, so don't blame me.'

'I can't understand it,' Celia cried, trotting after her. 'I honestly thought he loved you dearly.'

'Bah!' Georgina scoffed. 'Remember that word? *Now* what about your palm-reading and the big black dog?'

The big black dog appeared as she led Stardust round the side of the house. Prince bounded up, grinning at her and making Stardust back nervously. As far as Georgina was concerned, Prince was as bad as his master, and she glared at him.

'Get lost!' she yelled, and he whined in anxious surprise, dropping down and looking at her in astonishment. It quite touched her heart and she bent to stroke him.

'Oh, I'm sorry. It's not your fault that you got landed with a cruel, treacherous master. You'll never know, will you?'

When she looked up Steven was standing on the steps, his hands on his lean hips and his black frown permanently fixed. She looked right through him and then walked off, hoping like mad that every other member of the family would see her taking poor Stardust away to inferior quarters.

Of course, Celia didn't tell tales on her beloved brother even if she had dared, and nobody else seemed to notice. Georgina got up at six to exercise Stardust, being quite determined not to be caught out again. Her father took it all in his stride as usual, simply looking closely at her small determined face and murmuring, 'Oh, battling with Steven again, are you?'

Was she indeed? Life had been perfect before Steven came back; now each day was grim and bitter. And she would never give in. Never! Never! Gradually other people would find out what he was really like. Wasn't Celia discovering it now?

* * *

She continued to go out with Jeremy as a matter of self-preservation, although Mrs Ripley drove her close to homicide.

'You know there's no way I can get married yet, Georgina,' he told her quietly one evening on the way home from a dance. 'Mother isn't quite ready yet to face having another woman in the house.'

Georgina was taken aback. She felt an attack of panic threatening. Marriage was final. She hadn't thought of marriage and she had not really expected Jeremy to raise the subject for years yet.

'I didn't know you even contemplated it, Jeremy,' she got out hastily before he could go on. 'I know your mother thinks you're too young.'

'It's not really that, Georgina,' he said with a little laugh, taking her hand firmly. 'I think you intimidate her a bit. You're full of fighting spirit and she's not sure how you would take to the discipline of the farm.'

'Me? But I—I. . .' It was one thing for her to talk blithely to her father, and yet another to be faced with this off-beat offer of marriage—if that was what it was.

'You know I intend to marry you, Georgina,' he persisted seriously. 'You've always known what I have in mind. It's not my way to be showy and demonstrative, but I care about you.'

'I—I know you do. You're a really good friend.'

'Well, then. That's what a marriage should be. Really good friends for a lifetime. Farming is hard work and it's essential that a couple should think along the same lines. One of the things is that you've got to learn to curb that tongue a bit. Mother's quite worried how you'll turn out.'

'Is she honestly? That's good of her—I didn't know she cared so much.' Georgina felt hysteria rising like a great cloud. A lovely safe marriage. The best of friends. With Mrs Ripley to watch her and teach her some discipline. What did they think got her up each day and kept her working until late each evening but discipline? She almost choked at the thought of them mulling over her good and bad points as if she were a prize pig. 'Truly I think I've already "turned out". You can't change people at my age.'

'Really, you're so funny, so dramatic, Georgina,' he laughed. 'You're only a young girl yet. Both of us are years from marriage. Mother agrees with that and you've got to admit she's right.'

'She is,' Georgina conceded. 'Still, I don't know. I don't feel much like a young girl.' She gave a great sigh, her natural exuberance rising to the top at the thought of his mother standing guard over her with those folded arms. 'I've had several passionate affairs.'

She instantly wished she hadn't said that, even to shock Jeremy, because all it did was bring back the memory of being in Steven's arms. The only passionate affairs had been in her mind, all with Steven. Jeremy was duly shocked, surprising her by grabbing her arms.

'If I didn't know you love to say wicked things I'd be furious, Georgina. You never know when to stop, do you?'

No, she didn't. Her tongue constantly got her into trouble with everyone, and Steven didn't laugh at it any more.

'It's all talk, Jeremy,' she said quietly. 'I don't know why I say things like that.'

'Yes, well, try to control yourself,' he suggested sternly. 'You can see now why I think you're too young yet? One day you'll have to stop all this and grow up. Until then we'll just go on as we are.' He suddenly smiled and pulled her into his arms. 'Don't worry. I'll take care of you, Georgina.'

She didn't need anyone to take care of her and she almost told him, because she was beginning to get angry, but Steven's face rose to the top of her mind, his blue eyes serious, unsmiling, and she could still hear his voice.

'*I* took care of you.'

Not any more, though. Now she was committed to fight him.

She continued to work like a slave, determined to give Steven not one chance to get at her, because she knew he watched her progress with deadly interest, even though he never spoke to her. Her father noticed too and it worried him.

'Well, there's never been much of you, but what there is is disappearing,' he said grimly one morning. 'I don't know what's got into you but I know there's something. You're up at six and never in bed until eleven. I'm hard pressed to find anything to do around here. Each time I look round it's done.'

She couldn't tell him. Like everyone else, he thought Steven was wonderful, and if he knew she had been told to work harder he would stalk up to the hall and have it all out with Steven, thereby causing more trouble.

Being robbed of her morning ride and gossip, Celia took to coming down to the Dower House more regularly, and in that way Georgina kept up with the news, because she never set foot in the place, putting off Lady Evelyn's mild complaints by pleading pressure of work with the new season.

It saddened her terribly because she missed them and she missed her happy days at the hall. Also, she was lying. Steven had made her into as much of a liar as he was himself.

CHAPTER SIX

A FEW days later Jeremy surprised Georgina by appearing on the estate. She had left the Land Rover parked by the gate and walked down the hill to see how the men had got on with the thinning in the wood. For reasons best known to themselves they had left a great fallen tree just on the edge, out into the field. Unless she could see any good reason for it they could get themselves back and remove it this afternoon. She was standing contemplating it when she heard Jeremy calling. He had parked and was walking to meet her.

'What brings you here?' She walked back to him and stood with her hands in the pockets of her jeans, a vivid picture of light and colour with her red hair gleaming and her green sweater clinging to her small tilted breasts. She had left her jacket in the car and hoped he didn't intend to keep her talking. It was a bit chilly, even in the sun. She was pleased to see him, though. She was so lonely nowadays that the sight of Jeremy was really good.

'Good neighbourliness,' he informed her in his usual serious way. 'Did you know the river is rising quickly?'

'Not really. I haven't had the chance to get over that way for a day or two.' She was worried at once. Sometimes in the spring the lower fields flooded. It all depended how much rain there had been in the hills, and if the river was rising there must have been plenty. It might be necessary to go round and alert the farms.

'Well, I was out this way and I thought I'd better let you know.' He smiled down at her. 'You've been so busy lately that I thought I'd try to see you and get you to go to the dance over at Carley tomorrow night,' he added when she said nothing at all.

Excuses sprang into her head straight away. She hadn't really the energy to get ready to go out at night nowadays, and it would mean a trip on the way to check up on the health and safety of Mrs Ripley, a thing that brought booming laughter from her father because, according to him, anyone who attacked Jeremy's mother was going to come out of it badly maimed.

'If she didn't kill them she'd lecture them to death,' he surmised.

She would probably lecture Georgina too. She usually did. It was getting a bit much and she knew, anyway, that all she felt for Jeremy was friendship.

'I'm not sure if I can, Jeremy. There's a lot to do.'

'I can't see why you have to do it,' he pointed out. 'You're not a farm worker. *We* don't have all the help that the Templetons do and we manage very nicely.'

His annoyance surprised her. She had never thought of anyone being jealous of the Templetons, especially not Jeremy. His farm was good and quite big, and he had plenty of men too.

'You don't have two estates here and one in Scotland to run,' Georgina reminded him. 'You've got one farm. There are three on this estate alone and fifteen spread over all the holdings. In any case, it's a business and I help to run it.'

'We all know about the Templeton Estates,' he grumbled. 'I bet they'd like our farm too.'

'Don't be ridiculous!' She stared at him in astonishment. 'They don't grab land, Jeremy.'

'They've already grabbed it,' he muttered.

'It's a business and a big one. Everybody works like mad.'

'Except Miss Celia Templeton. She does plenty of gadding about.'

Georgina didn't know what had brought this on but her ready temper rose. 'For your information, Celia is a trained secretary and puts in her stint with the rest, and I'd like to remind you that she's my friend.'

'She won't want to know you when you're married to a farmer,' Jeremy informed her. 'Mother saw you two shopping the other day. She was just saying to me that you'd be dropped like a hot cake when you married an ordinary farmer.'

'If I do!' Georgina said crossly. How she was keeping her temper at all she didn't know. It infuriated her to imagine Mrs Ripley mulling over *her* future. She was seeing a side of Jeremy that she had never seen before too.

'Now, Georgina. You know we'll get married, even if we don't speak about it.'

'I wonder why we don't speak about it?' she asked. Here he was, quietly and almost secretly planning her future, too sedate to even ask her opinion. Steven had simply threatened to take her, like the village squire and a maiden.

'It's not necessary,' he muttered. 'Heavens, we've been going steady for four years. Everyone expects it.'

Was that why he wanted to marry her, because everyone expected it? She had a wild picture of Steven asking her to marry him. No, he would *tell* her. He would just drag her along by the hand. She felt a shiver of dismay run over her skin. When Steven kissed her she was so completely lost. It was a life sentence, loving Steven. It made her doomed to be alone forever.

'Look, I don't mean to upset you,' Jeremy coaxed. 'It's just that you seem to be so involved with the Templetons, and it's just spoiling you for when you have to be an ordinary farmer's wife.'

'How do you know you want to marry me?' Georgina persisted miserably. 'You hardly ever kiss me properly. We might not be suited.'

'There's more to marriage than that.' He looked as if she was behaving badly again. 'Romance is fine in its place but there's compatibility and so many other things. When we're married——'

Georgina didn't even let him finish.

'Kiss me!' she ordered, glaring at him.

'Georgina! This is neither the time nor the place.'

Steven had said that when she'd been almost begging to belong to him. Steven! Steven! Damn him! He sneaked into her every thought, her every dream.

'I'm waiting,' she informed Jeremy fiercely, and he suddenly laughed, reaching across to her.

'Really, Georgina. I can't resist you. Sometimes you're a wonderful clown.'

He leaned over to peck at her cheek and she almost stamped with frustration. Before he could escape she flung her arms around his neck and pressed her mouth to his, kissing him soundly, opening her lips as she had never done before with him. He surprised her. His arms tightened round her and he kissed her back urgently.

That was when she wanted to get away with all speed. She didn't like it. When Steven kissed her she burned, floated away on molten wings, drifted exotically into another world. Now she wanted to struggle, but she had truly asked for this. It was a great relief when he suddenly drew back and looked down at her sternly.

'No, Georgina,' he said in a shaken voice. 'I'm not going to start kissing you like that because one thing leads to another and I have too much respect for you. You—you mustn't ever try to kiss me like that again— well, not until we're engaged officially.'

She was sorry, very sorry, but then, wasn't she always doing things she was sorry about? And Jeremy would be so embarrassed. He was, but his eyes had a gleam in them she hadn't seen before, and she knew she had done something very wrong and would have to stop seeing him. She couldn't let things drift like this. Maybe going away was not such a bad idea.

'I'm sorry, Jeremy,' she muttered. 'I don't know what came over me.'

'I never knew you felt like that, Georgina,' he said with a very red but very pleased look. 'Mother thinks you're a tomboy—of course, she likes you,' he added quickly. 'Don't worry that you wanted to kiss me so much. You're safe with me.'

She didn't tell him that it had been a disastrous experiment to see if anyone else could make her float off and, by the look on his face, Jeremy was going to keep it to himself. It wasn't something he would discuss with his mother.

'Will she let you get married, do you think?' she asked in a light-headed sort of way, having no idea how to continue except to say 'Well, goodbye, then'.

'Heavens, what a question! I'm only twenty-five. Years yet to think about that. We've got a lot of living to do before then.'

'You and your mother?' He had said it as if living would suddenly end when he was married. It would too— Mrs Ripley would be there.

'Don't be a tease, Georgina.' He frowned at her, back to lecturing, an inherited gift. 'I would never tease you.'

No, he wouldn't. His mother looked as if she would have to look the word up in a dictionary, and then she would disapprove. Steven used to tease all the time. When she was little he had teased her but he had always been there when she'd needed him. When she had begun to grow up she had never even thought of anyone but Steven. He had been in her every dream, her wonderful, handsome Steven.

'Look, I'll have to get on,' Jeremy said. 'Try to make it for the dance.' He gave her a little hug. 'Don't look so unhappy. I'm not cross with you—I know you're a bit impetuous, dear.'

Well, that was a step forward. His first sign of real passion. Still, he called his mother 'dear' too, so what the hell? She walked with him the rest of the way, which wasn't far, and her heart leapt like a wild thing as she saw Steven parked by the low hedge, the top of his car down now and a look on his face that warned her he might very well have been an interested spectator to the strange events of the last few minutes.

'Any problems?' he asked Jeremy.

'No. I just called to let Georgina know that the river's rising. All part of being a good neighbour.'

Steven said nothing. He just nodded, lifting his hand in an indolent farewell as Jeremy reversed and drove off. He slowed first, though, and looked meaningly at Georgina, and she suddenly knew he was suspicious of Steven. So was she. Flight was a good idea. She waved, and Jeremy looked more relaxed as he left.

Georgina didn't get the chance to flee. Steven lounged back in his seat, his arm on the door as he looked up at her quizzically.

'Didn't he fancy a love-scene, then?'

Colour flooded her face and her eyes sparkled warningly.

'You have no business to spy on us!'

'Spy on you? My dear George, I could see you a mile off. You were right out in the open. I can hardly be blamed for seeing you grab the poor, hapless soul and kiss him to death.' He was bitingly sarcastic and she noted that she was George again, which meant he was no longer so angry and giving himself some rope to hang her with. Her eyes darkened in embarrassment and he looked at her steadily.

'Making a comparison, were you?' he asked softly.

Yes, she had been, a disastrous comparison, and she was the more furious for it.

'How could Jeremy compare with you?' she seethed. 'He's a quiet, kind person, not a lecherous——'

The sapphire-blue eyes flashed like flames and he vaulted out of the car before she had even managed to finish the sentence, and she had no thought at all of standing up to him. She just turned and ran down the hill as fast as she could, making for the shelter of the woods, her heart in her mouth. Why, oh, why couldn't she keep her cool with Steven?

She had to manoeuvre herself round the fallen tree, and he caught her easily as she made it to the trees, swinging her round, furiously angry.

'There are some names I don't take from anyone,' he rasped, 'not even from a red-haired vixen!'

'You don't have to take anything, Mr Templeton, because I've finally made my mind up. I'm leaving. You'll get my resignation soon. I'll get another job until Jeremy and I get married.'

She had thought his hands too tight on her arms but now they tightened enough to stop the blood in her veins.

'So that's what it was about,' he grated. 'You were proposing to him?'

It made her feel stupid, foolish and terribly lost. She tried not to cry. Instead she pulled to get away but he shook her hard, and that just about did it. Tears came into her eyes in a great flood and coursed down her cheeks before she could stop them. He let her go and she just sat down on the grass under the trees, her head bent in misery. Life would seem very long without Steven in it. The days would be dark and endless, empty.

It took him a second to regain his temper, and then he was kneeling down by her, lifting her and seeing the blind anguish on her face.

'I've hurt you. Don't cry, Georgina. I'm sorry, really sorry, sweetheart.'

'You're not! You love hurting me,' she sobbed. 'You've always hurt me and you always will. And don't call me that!'

'I've always called you that,' he reminded her softly.

'When I was a child it was all right. It's not all right now.'

He had come down on the grass with her, lifted her up into his arms and now he looked into her frantically tragic face with serious blue eyes.

'Y-you've finally driven me away,' she went on wildly between sobs. 'You know how it will hurt my father. And—and he hates Mrs Ripley. He'll never come to see me. I'll h-have to meet Dad secretly.'

'Are they going to make a slave of you, Georgie?' His hand was cradling her head but she didn't seem to notice, and she didn't notice his blue-eyed amusement either.

'I—I'm to have more self-discipline,' she choked, lost in misery and at the moment quite believing it. The amusement faded from his face.

'The hell you are,' he grated. 'Nobody disciplines the Templetons.'

'I'm not one,' she sobbed.

'By mutual acquiescence you probably are.' His hand smoothed back her tumbled red hair. 'My mother loves you like her own.'

It was a bit of comfort. She was still giving muffled little sobs, not quite in control of herself or she wouldn't be lying here in his arms.

'Anyway,' she confessed sadly, 'I don't think I'm going to marry Jeremy. And if you say his mother wouldn't let him——'

'I wasn't going to. I think we've got enough mileage out of Jeremy.' He lifted her right into his arms, raising her higher, and she just came like a small creature trapped by fascination, her wide eyes luminous and searching, her flushed face paler now. 'Why aren't you marrying Jeremy?' he asked softly.

'I don't think he wants me, not really.'

'That's just as well. He can't have you.'

His eyes were on her soft, trembling lips and she felt as if the whole world was waiting, everything still and paused. Even her heart seemed to slow down.

'Why do you say things like that?' she whispered.

'You know damned well why. For the same reason you grabbed that poor creature and smothered him with kisses. It's called frustration, because this is what you want, what we both want.'

He lowered his dark head, his gaze holding hers until her eyes closed, and she seemed to float higher into his arms as his lips claimed hers.

Her instant response fired his desire more. From anger and tears she was bewitched, spellbound, ready for his lovemaking as if he had commanded it. Her light body was soft and trembling in his arms, every curve of her fitted close to him as if she was made for no other reason, and his arms tightened convulsively, his hand spearing into her thick hair and bringing her mouth closer.

She had always been tempestuous, flashing golden eyes, gleaming red hair, a radiant, shining creature, almost part of the wind and sky. He had wanted this wild, bright girl for years and his own recent temper had left him almost dangerously aroused.

'Open your mouth,' he ordered against her lips.

Strangely enough she had kept her lips closed, still remembering Jeremy's remarks that had made her feel slightly cheap, and she drew back to look at him.

'Why?' He looked frustrated and puzzled but she persisted, worrying away at it as if it was terribly important. 'Why must I open my mouth?'

His fingers trailed across her cheek and his thumb
found her lips and probed the corner, his eyes on the
sweet, soft curve of them.

'Because when you open your mouth you're saying
yes to me,' he told her huskily. 'Say yes to me, Georgie.'

Her lips parted instantly, a cushioned softness against
his masculine power, and he took them fiercely, draining
her willing sweetness, his own cool control almost en-
tirely gone. She seemed to quiver in his arms, a spasm
of erotic delight, and he lowered her to the grass, his
body half covering hers. There was no way she would
be close enough unless she was lying naked in his arms,
he thought blindly. His desire for her was now like a
fire, white-hot.

Her slender arms wound around his neck, her fingers
finding the shining black of his hair, and she felt the
tremendous tension in him that curbed the drive to
subdue her and claim her. She never thought beyond the
moment. She was back with Steven, crushed to him, the
taste of him in her mouth, and she responded urgently,
feeling the triumphant shudder that raced through him.
It was Steven, holding her close, every dream she had
ever had.

She murmured against his lips, her slight body beginning to move instinctively against him, and desire
seemed to fly in sparks from his fingers as his hands
sought her breasts, fiercely pushing her soft sweater
away, the dominant male, intent and impassioned. She
felt his mouth on her body, hotly on her breasts and on
the slender tension of her stomach, and she moved more
wildly, heated little cries pouring from her until he
crushed them with his own lips.

The anger they had both felt before, her hot tears and
his determination to punish her, had driven them both
into a sensual madness, making them unaware of anything but the taste and feel of each other. She seemed

to have waited all her life for this, the powerful, sleek body over her own, the urgent hands and mouth. The sexual rapture flooded over her, carrying her away on clouded wings.

'Steven! Steven!' She murmured his name over and over like someone in the deep thrall of ecstasy as his lips traced her skin and he moved back to her trembling mouth, hungry for the taste of it, knowing every danger but powerless to deny himself. He was more tender now, his lips fused with hers, moving against her with sweet compulsion, his strong hands trembling as they traced her body with slow, powerful strokes.

The zip of her jeans was pushed down and she felt a great burst of joy, no fear at all, not with Steven. She had never wanted anyone else, would never want anyone else. Her hips just seemed to lift by themselves, moulding her to him, and he gave a great, shuddering sigh, knowing they were on the very edge of belonging.

'Oh, God! This is madness!' He buried his face between her breasts and she cried out, a heartbroken plea.

'Don't stop, Steven! Don't leave me!'

They were words from long ago, words from her eighteenth birthday when he had kissed her into a blaze of flame. They echoed in her head and memory came, returning reason and a great desolation.

'Don't!' he warned sharply, attuned to her every mood, looking down into her eyes, eyes that were now wide open and accusing. 'Don't throw us headlong back into that.'

She shut him out, closing her eyes tightly, her body now taut and unwilling, disclaiming him. She lay there quite still for a moment while he watched her closely, his own breathing not yet under control, and then suddenly she went wild, her volatile nature exploding into despairing anger, her small fists beating at his chest, aiming for his dark, imperious face.

'Did you have nothing better to do today? Isn't there anyone else available but the hired help?' Tears of pain and frustration filled her honey-gold eyes. 'It's not too far to London if you start now.'

He caught her wildly moving hands, trapping them in his, holding her arms painfully over her head.

'Stop it!' he ordered. 'I've had enough. You're not the only one aching inside. You wanted me to take you here, like this, while the merry country-folk cheered? I saw you and Ripley a mile off. You imagine we're invisible because we want each other?'

'Oh!' Unable to move, she shook her bright head from side to side, rage sparking through the tears. 'The droit de seigneur must be taken at the castle?'

'I've told you to stop!' he said dangerously. He slowly let her go, watching her carefully, expecting her to leap up and race off in this wild, hurt mood, but she was too spent to even lower her arms, lying like a tiny doll as he slowly straightened her clothes.

Clearly she was not going to move at all. He saw she was more subdued, her temper dying, a terrible, innocent bewilderment taking its place, and he brought her arms down to her sides and then lifted her to her feet, steadying her when she swayed.

'You're a cruel brute,' she murmured shakily. 'A pig, even.'

'That's right, but don't push your luck. Remember where that just got you.'

'I couldn't care less.' Still unable to even breathe properly, she sank back to defiance.

'We've just disproved that. Come along.' He got his arm round her and led her back up to the road, and slowly common sense returned. From here you could see and be seen for miles. He was perfectly right.

'I'm sorry,' she muttered, her head bent.

'Again,' he added grimly. 'Repeat after me, "I am not fit to be let out".'

'I am not fit to be let out,' she intoned solemnly, and he led her to his car, pushing her inside.

'What about the Land Rover? What about the tree? I have things to do and then there's the river and——'

'*Shut up!*' Steven ordered forcefully. 'You will truly drive me mad. The Land Rover stays where it is until I get around to it. Like most things, it's mine.'

'That's right,' she agreed, ignoring the innuendo. 'You're the boss now.'

'Sir! You forgot to say sir. Isn't that what I am now?'

In spite of their frantic lovemaking he looked a bit grim, and she thought it best to be quiet.

'Where are we going?' she asked after a while when she dared to question him, and it became apparent that they were about to leave the estate.

'I'm going to the village and I'm taking you with me.'

'I look a mess.'

'Kissed to pieces but not a mess. Your new image is stunning.'

'Is that why you kissed me?'

'Step carefully,' he warned softly. 'Remember you're with a cruel, untrustworthy brute, still miles from anywhere.'

It made her shiver a little and she dived headlong into a new conversation.

'Where's Prince?'

'The treacherous dog of a treacherous master?' He looked grim again and she turned to him beseechingly.

'I thought this was some sort of truce? How can we have a truce if you keep on saying things like that?'

'It won't last long. I'm aware you don't trust me one inch, Georgina, when that odd little brain starts working, but we'll try for the truce.'

'All right, then. Where's Prince?' It was no use saying she trusted him, because she didn't. There was no getting around the fact that he was having an affair with Auriel.

'I don't always bring him. He wants more than his fair share of everything. He'd like to drive but I threaten him.'

It made her laugh and she glanced across at him, her heart in her eyes if he could have seen.

'Sometimes I adore you,' she said softly.

'But mostly you distrust me,' he added. 'Here we are.' He swept into the village, acknowledging greeting with a wave of the hand, and she bit her lip when she realised she wanted to be here, right beside him, for always. At this moment Auriel seemed distant, unimportant. She could still taste his kisses.

He insisted on taking her into the tea-rooms for a cup of tea, and she gradually relaxed because when Steven set out to charm he could play on her feelings like a master musician. She was almost eating out of his hand. She had loved him all her life, and just being with him was magic.

Later she sat in the car and waited while he went into the post office, and that was when Jeremy drove up. He was just about to drive past when he saw her. There was no mistaking that deep red hair, and he jammed on the brakes, reversing and getting out to tower over the car.

'What are you doing here in that car?' he asked angrily.

'I'm with Steven. We came for a cup of tea.' She refused to feel guilty, not when he was glaring at her as if he had every right to do it.

'I don't like it, even if you do work for him. You're my girl and I'll feel an utter fool if anyone sees you here with him.'

'Look, Jeremy, I'm sorry but...' It was the time to tell him but she didn't get the chance. Steven came up, his eyes frosty as he saw her flushed face. He just nodded at Jeremy and got into the car, starting the engine. His lips were in one straight line and he looked as if he was going to drive off without a word.

'I'll talk to you at the dance tomorrow night,' Jeremy said tightly.

'I'm afraid not. Georgina is going out with me.' Steven just drove off, leaving Jeremy scowling after them, and Georgina was almost open-mouthed.

'Why did you do it? Why did you? It will be all over the village by morning. Jeremy tells his mother everything.'

'Good,' Steven said with satisfaction. 'It will keep her busy. We've seen enough of that youth, I think.'

'Will you stop that? He's twenty-five!'

'So be it. A twenty-five-year-old youth. Drop him.'

'You can't say that!'

'Strange, I imagined I already had,' Steven murmured sardonically. 'I have good reasons. In the first place, I brought you up to certain high standards, and Ripley does not measure up, with or without his mother. You are Celia's friend and my mother's delight; neither of them could even contemplate visiting you if you became the young Mrs Ripley. Jeremy's mother quite puts them off, not to mention Jeremy himself. You will recall that Harry would not even manage a visit. That would leave you alone, to be disciplined!' He turned to frown at her and then looked back at the road. 'Secondly, your new image deserves better than a farmer's hop. You will go out with me to sophisticated places; it's what you're used to. I trained you for it.'

'I think I've got a virus,' Georgina said wildly. 'I keep hearing words but they don't make any sense. You can't mean all this?'

'I most certainly do. In future you're going out with me, regularly. At least until young Jeremy is vanquished.'

'I refuse!' Georgina stated, quelling her mad heart-beats when he made it clear that this was definitely a temporary measure to reorganise her life to his satisfaction. 'I've never heard such stupid, snobbish reasons.'

'I am not a snob, as you know full well,' Steven said calmly, turning on to the estate and driving along the narrow lanes. 'It's a matter of the rightness of things. I've always known what was right for you. Besides, there's another reason—the main one, actually.'

'Well, let's hope it's more sensible than the other two.'

'It is. You're going out with me because I want you. I mean to have you, and not wildly and instantly beside the wood.'

She was suddenly silent, unnerved, and without any answer for the first time in her life. Was this Steven, her childhood idol, her dream lover, planning to seduce her with methodical coldness? She tried to sink into her seat, to disappear, but nothing could camouflage her white face, her bewildered wide eyes, her shining dark red hair that blew around her. He glanced across at her and then at her tightly clenched hands.

'There's no need to be nervous,' he murmured quietly. 'I'll make you happy. You'll wake up in my arms. I know you want to, so don't start any schoolgirl machinations.'

It was worse than ever, outside her experience. If he said anything else she was sure she would faint. She could feel herself sinking lower into the seat.

'We'll give it a while, shall we? Time for you to get used to the thought,' he asked casually. 'If we still fight bitterly then I'll go away again. There's plenty of family business to run. As it is, I'll have to be away quite frequently. If this battle still rages to the death then I'll move back to my London flat.'

Where there were plenty of willing women and, no doubt, Auriel. She was trembling so much that she couldn't stop.

'I—I don't believe all this. It's a terrible thing to say.'

'Terrible? Georgina, not long ago it was exactly what you wanted. You begged me not to stop. I've wanted you for a long time.'

'Y—you haven't,' she whispered, afraid to look at him. 'Please, Steven, don't talk like this. I—I feel strange.'

'You think I'm teasing? It's not the sort of thing I tease about. It's deadly serious and you've wanted me for an uneasily long time too. You were barely sixteen when that look in your eyes was all too obvious, hero worship to desire. Why do you think I packed you off to school with Celia? I could see it coming a mile off. You were too young, my sweet, still almost unbearably young at eighteen. You're a woman now and the most passionate little thing I've ever held. I've waited long enough for you.'

'I—I don't know exactly what you mean,' she whispered. 'Are—are you proposing to me?'

She went even paler still when he laughed.

'Proposing to you? No, I don't think so. Marriage isn't what I have on my mind at the moment.'

She looked up at the cool sunlit sky as if she had never seen it before. The familiar trees flashed past, new and fresh for the spring. Her face was a small tragedy and she was too stunned to fight now. She had imagined him telling her to marry him. He was telling her to be his mistress, and that only on a local basis.

'Don't be frightened.' He took her cold hand and raised it to his lips. 'Haven't I always taken care of you? I'll make you very happy, sweetheart.'

And terribly she knew he would—if she gave in.

Georgina was still completely silent as they drew up outside the Dower House. She couldn't look at Steven.

She would never be able to look at him again. Now she wanted to leave Kellerdale Hall, to run as far and as fast as she could. She felt bewildered and endangered. This was no underhand plot. It was all out in the open, the rules laid down squarely.

Steven was perfectly normal. He got out to open the door for her and handed her out courteously, and of course he would—his new mistress. He could hardly call her the local madwoman now. He didn't move aside and she stared with terrible attention at his sweater, not raising her eyes higher than the power of his chest.

'No more work today,' he ordered quietly. 'I'll deal with the Land Rover and pass out messages about the river.'

When she didn't answer he tilted her face, looking into her bewildered eyes.

'I'll call for you at eight. We're going to dinner and a nightclub. I like the green dress.'

'Yes, Steven.' It was beyond her to say anything else. Of course, she could have shouted loudly and refused, but the awful thing was that she didn't want to. She was utterly devoid of will, some weak extension of Steven.

His soft laughter seemed to shiver down her spine, and the hand on her chin moved to caress her face.

'You'll get used to it. Sometimes perhaps we'll even fight a little. I'm not going to rush you.' He bent his head, his lips stroking across her unresisting mouth, and then he let her go. 'Eight o'clock,' he reminded her, and drove off.

She walked into the house in a daze. I'm a shadow, she thought. I don't really exist. Everything in life has really been a dream and it's all slowed down—limbo. Her father was out and she was glad there was nobody about to see her. Not that they would have seen her. She wasn't real. If she looked in the mirror she wouldn't be there. She avoided it carefully.

In the kitchen the cup and saucer rattled in her hand and she looked down at them in surprise, astonished that she could hear the noise. Even a cup of tea did nothing to bring her back to reality. She would be able to think when Steven told her to think. Until then she was without purpose, undirected, aimless—a ghost.

CHAPTER SEVEN

EVEN as Georgina got ready she knew no reality. Steven wanted the green dress—that much she could remember. She was even avoiding her own father. When he came home she had shouted down that she was going out, very relieved that he could hear her phantom voice. It gave her the courage to look in the mirror, but she had to look away again. Her eyes seemed to be too big for her face, her glowing hair the only thing about her that was real.

'Glad you're going out,' her father said as she came down into the drawing-room. 'I'm having dinner with Jim Betchely. Met him at the auction yesterday.' He turned round and stopped dead in his tracks. 'Heavens, love. Are you all right?'

'Perfectly.' She managed a bright smile, certain it would look all wrong, like a scarecrow with lipstick.

'I've never seen you looking so lovely, but you're pale, too pale. Tell that young Ripley to get you home early. Wherever is he taking you to justify that beautiful dress?'

'I—I'm going out with Steven.' She felt she was almost whispering it, and her father's face softened.

'Ah! That explains it.'

She didn't know what he meant, but he was suddenly very kind, and when she heard the car she felt like asking him to come along too.

There was nothing furtive about Steven. He came straight into the house as he had done all her life.

'I suppose you've heard about the river, Harry? I passed the message around, so if anyone gets their stock trapped they've only themselves to blame.'

'Even the beck's rising. Noticed it on my way in,' her father said seriously. 'Could be bad this year.'

They were both so normal that Georgina said nothing at all. Her eyes were huge, glowing with wild thoughts like saying, 'Daddy, I'm going to be Steven's mistress. I'd like you to be the first to know.'

Steven was smiling at her; his eyes softened and he put out his hand.

'Come on, Sunflower. I've booked the table.'

She just put her hand in his and went where he led, feeling she was floating beside him. She couldn't feel the cold air or anything, and Steven opened the car door for her, looking down at her in the moonlight.

' "Full beautiful, a faery's child," ' he quoted softly. He kissed her cheek gently. 'I really believe you need a strong drink.'

The first thing he did was order her a brandy as they waited for their table, and at least it put a bit of colour into her face. People seemed to be staring at her, and Steven caught her anxious looks.

'Everyone likes to stare at a beautiful girl,' he murmured, drawing her close to his side. 'Don't look around for a stick.'

As if she could. *That* Georgina seemed to have gone, gone forever. This one would disappear into a drift of smoke if anyone spoke to her.

Over dinner Steven was wonderful to her, keeping her entertained, directing her gently back to her food when her appetite failed. Later they watched the floor show as they drank coffee, and then they went to the casino, a place she had never even dreamed of. The exciting atmosphere caught her immediately and she was per-

suaded to have a small try, sitting at one of the tables
as Steven stood behind, directing her.

Gradually her fear left her, especially as she had a
couple of small wins, and she found herself turning her
face back to look up at Steven for approval, her colour
normal, her eyes shining.

'I won!'

'I know. Don't get hooked.' He smiled down at her
and for a second their glances locked. Oh, she was
hooked, but it wasn't with gambling and he knew it. She
turned swiftly away for one last go, her fingers trembling now, and after a second she felt his hands come
to her shoulders, moving slowly and almost impercep-
tibly on her satin skin, his thumbs gently caressing her
nape beneath her heavy hair until she melted inside and
wanted to just turn into his arms and be carried away.

She was driven home after midnight, hours after
Jeremy would have been in bed, and she felt like a wicked
lady, glamorous, pursued and desired. All the way Steven
kept up an amusing conversation until she almost forgot
why she was out with him.

She could see that her father was in bed. His car was
there and the lights were out, all except the one in the
hall. Steven drew up quietly outside and looked across
at her, and she began to tremble all over again. He
reached over and tilted her face, his fingers against her
smooth cheek.

'Kiss your date goodnight,' he ordered softly, leaning
across to brush her lips with his. Her lips trembled open,
she just couldn't help it, and his mouth lingered against
hers, just lightly touching.

'Want me?' he breathed into her mouth, and she could
neither shake her head nor answer.

He lifted his head, looking at her, his hand circling
her beautiful throat, his eyes holding her wide gaze.

'Don't be frightened. I'll never hurt you.' His smiling eyes roamed all over her face. 'Did you enjoy tonight?'

'Yes, thank you, Steven.' She could only manage a whisper, and his smile lingered.

'You're afraid. When I take you I want it to be a joy, not a terror. You're beautiful. Goodnight, Georgina.'

He kissed her quickly and then got out to open the door for her.

'Lock the house,' he ordered with a sudden grin. 'We don't want anyone stealing Harry.'

When she got to the door he called softly to her and she turned to look back, almost bemused to see how handsome he looked, how virile and intent. Steven! The only man she would ever want.

'In the morning,' he ordered softly, 'bring Stardust back home to the stables. I want to ride with you, but I suppose that's Celia's pleasure.'

'Stardust seems to be settled here,' she said a bit anxiously.

'She knows where she belongs. So do you. I'll ring you tomorrow.' Long after he had gone she stood in the hall; she was still dreamy but she was alive again. He had been wonderful to her. He *would* marry her, she knew it! She slept deeply, all her dreams of Steven, but then, they always had been.

'Gina! You're back!' Celia waited for her as she galloped up and then leaned across to hug her. 'I didn't wait. I thought our rides were over. Has Steven relented?'

'Yes.' She moved in beside Celia as they trotted up the rise. At this moment she didn't want any questions, but it was always difficult with Celia. Discretion and Celia did not go hand in hand.

'You've got little purple shadows under your eyes. I've never seen that before. Did Jeremy keep you out late?

I phoned at ten and your father said you were still out. I thought Jeremy retired early?'

'I wasn't out with Jeremy.'

Don't ask anything else, she prayed. Don't find out until you have to. But Celia was in a sparkling mood and she turned on Georgina gleefully.

'You've found somebody else! Saints be praised! I can't stand Jeremy.'

'He's not too keen on you,' Georgina informed her smartly, hoping to side-track her. It only worked for a second.

'He's actually said so? The cheek! He's wanting to turn you into a dull-as-ditchwater wife and he knows I disapprove. I was dreading a marriage in that direction. So who is it? Who did you go out with? Tell me about him at once!'

Left with no alternative, she had to tell the truth. It would all be known sooner or later. Steven wasn't about to keep it a deadly secret he had called for her at home and chatted with her father.

'I went out with Steven. We had dinner and then went to a casino.' She tried to make it matter-of-fact, but even the mention of his name was like an aphrodisiac and her face flushed.

Celia reined in and stared at her intently, and then began to smile.

'Oh! Oh! Oh!' she crowed. 'He was whistling this morning, the glares quite gone. I see a handsome stranger with a big black dog.'

'I see a raving lunatic with a big black eye,' Georgina said hotly. 'Will you stop all that? This is a truce, a temporary truce.'

What else could she say? If Celia knew her brother's plans she would faint clean away. Lady Evelyn would perish.

'Well, you're riding, aren't you? I bet Stardust is coming back to her stall.'

'She isn't. The truce might be very temporary indeed, and I'm not going through all that again.'

Right then and there she decided to defy Steven's order. If she gave him an inch he would take a million miles. She was going to keep Stardust right out of this, sneakily if necessary. She didn't suppose he inspected the stables every day, counting heads. There was no need to let him know just how deeply under his thumb she was.

'Well, Steven looks happy and that makes a nice change,' Celia stated, seeing danger in the honey-gold eyes. She started off again up the rise and Georgina followed, moving alongside. 'Auriel is extremely miffed nowadays. I really don't know how she has the nerve to be so nasty to us in our own house. Malcolm looks as if he's planning a major war and doesn't know how to start, and Steven is—peculiar. Something's brewing. The vat is coming to the boil.'

Georgina felt a waft of cold come over her skin. Steven could out-plan anybody. Was she mixed up in some long-term scheme? Had it to do with Auriel?

'Is Arnold coming up this weekend?' she asked quickly, to change the subject, and had the satisfaction of seeing Celia blush too.

'I don't think so. He's very busy, you know. He rang last night and said he might get up next weekend.'

'I see a dark stranger with a job in London,' Georgina said slyly, and Celia burst into laughter.

'I like him a lot, Gina. He's so much fun. I think he likes me too. Don't hit him again. I'd resent it.' It quite startled Georgina to remember she had been so full of fire just a short while ago. Now she was full of doubts and trepidation, longing to see Steven and dreading it.

'Arnold will certainly get up for the Easter ball,' Celia said, and Georgina's heart sank. She had forgotten that. At Easter there was always a charity ball at Kellerdale Hall. The whole family fell to, heart and soul, and Georgina did too, for as long as she could remember. It made money for the local hospital; and just about everyone came. This year it would be so different. By then she might be different herself: Steven might be her lover. She would never be able to resist him. If anyone else had said that to her she would either have collapsed with laughter or aimed fierce blows at their head.

With Steven it was different. If he continued as he had started last night she was lost. She had been floating on air this morning just remembering his gentleness. She felt mixed up, a cross between a scarlet woman and an innocent victim. And Auriel was still there, waiting for Steven. Nothing would sort itself out.

'Race you!' Celia cried, filled with exhilaration at the thought of Arnold and, for a wonder, she won, reining in sharply at the edge of the woods.

'I've got a plan!' she shouted gleefully.

'Count me out,' Georgina stated firmly, dragged from her inward qualms. 'I was a victim of your last plan.'

'It's about Malcolm and the Easter ball. Invite Rowena. She tickles Mal to death. He might just fall for her this time.'

'And what does he do with Auriel—take her out and lose her?'

'Things have a habit of working out,' Celia said comfortably, her own affairs being in order.

'Ha! Ha!' Georgina laughed mirthlessly. Things had a habit of ensnaring her. She wasn't sure either if Malcolm was up to any sort of battle with the likes of Auriel, and if he got rid of Auriel Steven would have a clear field.

'Invite her and see,' Celia pleaded.

'No!' This is not for Malcolm, she thought guiltily, it's for me. I don't want to lose Steven.

'I'll keep on at you.' Celia turned away a bit smugly, another plan to work on. Celia had always been big on plans, even when they were children, but it had usually been Georgina who had borne the brunt of the failures.

As they neared the hall Prince came bounding out and Georgina's heart started to hammer. It meant that Steven was close by because Prince never left him unless ordered back. When they rode into the stable-yard he was there, talking to Joe.

He came over, his hand on Stardust's silken mane.

'Have a nice ride?' He stood looking up at Georgina, his blue eyes gleaming, and all she could do was nod like a simpleton. She got that slow smile and he held up his arms. 'Going to get down, then?'

What could she do? She just slid off straight into his arms, and for a second he held her. She could almost hear Celia bubbling with glee but there wasn't a thing she could do about it.

Steven let her go with so much reluctance that she blushed brightly, and Celia threw her reins to Joe.

'Unsaddle for me, Joe, then I'll not tell anyone you dye your hair.'

'Cheeky madam!' Joe laughed, taking the reins more firmly. 'That Miss Celia's a real card,' he added as Celia walked off grinning.

She was making herself scarce quite obviously, and Georgina thought some explanation was due.

'I had to tell her we went out last night,' she murmured, avoiding Steven's eyes. Joe had gone off laughing to himself and they were alone for a minute.

'Had to tell her?' He tilted her chin with one imperious finger, looking down into her eyes. 'It's no secret, is it? Pretty soon it will be quite clear to everyone that you're going out with me and not Jeremy.'

'I—I didn't know if you wanted anyone to know. I thought——'

'Didn't I call for you last night? I'll be calling for you tonight too.'

'Are we going out?' She looked up quickly, her pleasure so real and so instant that he linked his hands behind her, holding her in the loose circle of his arms.

'We are, but this time I'll have you in earlier. There are dark little shadows under your eyes. No big deeds today, OK?'

Auriel came into the yard while they were still standing looking at each other, and her shriek of laughter was like a knife on a tin plate.

'Oh, Steven! Whatever is this? Are you playing the wicked squire?'

It struck home very deeply indeed with Georgina and she stiffened at once, her foolish happiness draining away. She felt an answering stiffness in Steven but it was anger. He turned and looked at Auriel, tucking Georgina in the curve of his shoulder.

'Didn't you get the message? I thought you knew Georgina was my girl.'

'Since when?' She was still scornfully amused, not quite sure if this was a joke or not, and Steven looked down at Georgina.

'How long have I known you?'

'About seventeen years,' she said shakily, so very unsure of herself now, no fire left.

'There you are. Since then,' he told Auriel, who now had no idea at all what to say. He turned Georgina and kissed the tip of her nose. 'In case I don't see you before, I'll pick you up at seven tonight. If we go out earlier you can get to bed before midnight. I don't want to see you tired.'

She escaped—there was no other word for it—and Steven was so furious with Auriel that he didn't seem to notice that Georgina took Stardust with her. So he was staking his claim openly? In a way it thrilled her, but she knew what nobody else knew, after all. He wanted her for a mistress and nothing more. It was a shame and an excitement and a tragedy all at the same time.

Maybe even that was a lie, she mused after a little more thought. Celia said he was behaving peculiarly, and hadn't that little scene at the stable been quite out of character for Steven? Auriel had been furious. Was that the general idea, to make her see what she was missing?

By the end of the week she was utterly bewildered. Steven had taken her out almost every night, had entertained her, looked after her and gently kissed her goodnight. She didn't know where she was any more but she was walking on air, refusing to think further than the one day at a time. At the back of her mind she was aware that Auriel would know he was out every night and where he was, but she wouldn't let it make her miserable. She was with Steven and it would have to do for now. Maybe it would have to do forever.

At the end of the week he went to London and she missed him unbearably. The thought of any other woman with him hurt like a real pain. She could do nothing but work to take her mind off it, and on Saturday evening Celia came down to have dinner with her. She too was gloomy. Arnold couldn't get away and she was missing him.

'Auriel's running riot, you know,' she said as they curled up with coffee before the drawing-room fire. 'Malcolm is more or less ignoring her. It's extraordinary. Sometimes he behaves as if he's never seen her before and she's been watching Steven this week as if he might just turn into a devil.'

'She knows I'm going out with him,' Georgina confessed, and Celia smiled and patted her hand.

'Are you honestly? Is it a definite thing, then? I've always known how you feel about Steven. These battles have only really been camouflage.' She leaned back with a sigh. 'How beautifully things are working out. You and Steven, Arnold and me. We just have to get rid of Auriel,' she concluded, drumming her shining finger-nails against the arm of the settee. 'How to do it, though? I was rather banking on Rowena.'

'Oh, don't, Celia,' Georgina pleaded. 'No more plans.'

'But, darling, I've got to see to Mal. He's my brother. We'll all be so happy. You married to Steve, Arnold and me...' She suddenly stopped when she saw Georgina's face. 'Anyway,' she added, 'we've got a bit of peace for a couple of days. Tomorrow Auriel is going back down to London—another job apparently.'

Georgina nearly cried then. Auriel was going to Steven. It was blindingly obvious—surely Celia could fathom that out? She felt so much older than Celia nowadays, no longer the fiery, light-hearted girl. Before the summer came it would all be over, settled, and in her heart she knew that Steven would end up with the woman he wanted. Desperately she knew it would not be her.

During the weekend the river rose so high that it trickled over its banks in a few places, and it rained quite a lot too. Forewarned as they were, they had moved the stock to higher ground, but her father was grumpy.

'I've never known it to be fine for the show,' he complained. 'All that work and it pours at least two days out of the four.'

He was talking about the agricultural show that was held each year at a town a few miles away. It drew buyers from all over the country and the various events made it a splendid day out. It was a big country fair, too, with stalls and events for the children, and Georgina usually went one day out of the four to see the horse-jumping. Her father and Sir Graham went each day. They were both stewards and, in any case, they always had their eyes open for any likely buys. The best of the stock from the county came to the show.

On Monday morning Steven rang, and just the sound of his voice made Georgina weak. She had to sit down.

'I can't get back until tomorrow,' he told her. 'Arnold and I have a few things to iron out here. Something unexpected came up.'

She couldn't answer breezily because she knew why he was staying: Auriel had managed to get down there. She knew it was the only real reason he had gone.

'Georgina? Are you still there?' When she didn't answer his voice sharpened, and she quickly got a hold on her miserable thoughts.

'Yes, I'm here. I'll see you tomorrow, then?'

'Of course you will,' he said softly, and tears came into her eyes. His voice was caressing her from so far away. She had no doubt that he wanted her, but how many other women did he want? Did he speak like that to all of them?

'It's been raining here. Has it rained in London?'

She couldn't think of anything else to say to him and she heard him laugh, that soft laughter that raced down her spine.

'Are we falling back on that good old standby, the weather?'

'I—I thought you might want to know. The river spilled over a bit more.'

'I'm grateful for the information but it's not what I wanted to know. Are you missing me?' His voice was low and seductive and her fingers tightened around the phone. She really thought she would die when he finally left her, and he would leave her. She would be a discarded mistress one day. She was so young and her life would be ruined.

'Georgina?'

'Yes. I'm missing you.' She almost whispered it and then felt a terrible desire to see him. She wanted to see him *now*. She couldn't bear him to be with Auriel.

'Come back, Steven! Please come back.' She couldn't hide the catch in her voice and clearly he heard it too.

There was an almost imperceptible pause and then his voice came again, warm and quiet. 'Tomorrow, sweetheart. As soon as I can. It might be late. We'll drive straight out and have a meal at a little country pub. We won't even waste time dressing up.'

When he said goodbye she just lay back on the settee and stared at the ceiling. She loved him so completely that nothing else ever mattered. When he finally reached for her she would simply melt into his arms. There was and only ever had been Steven. There would never be anyone else. Her fights with him had always been a battle with her own desire.

When Celia rang she sounded so gloomy that Celia briskly took matters in hand.

'On with the plastic mac,' she ordered. 'What's a bit of rain? We'll go to the show.'

'I've really got things to do.'

'Leave them. Who's to complain? Steven's in charge now and he adores you.' Temporarily, Georgina thought bleakly. Temporarily. And he didn't even adore her anyway, he just wanted her. There was no future really. Anyone with any sense at all would simply go away, leave the district, but she was trapped by a love that had grown since she was a child.

The rain cleared quite quickly and a rather watery sun shone as they arrived at the show-ground, although it was still a bit soggy underfoot. They leaned against the fence and watched the jumping, chatting with people they had always known, but Georgina felt out of it, slightly removed from reality as if she were watching herself from a long way off. When some acquaintance lured Celia away for a minute Georgina had to stifle the urge to cling to her arm. She had come to this! She was no longer even able to stick up for herself.

That was when Jeremy appeared, and he looked down at Georgina with very hard eyes.

'I've been waiting for her to go,' he announced grimly. 'I've been watching you for at least half an hour. I want to talk to you.'

'Well, here I am,' Georgina said gaily, deciding to ignore his tone and pretend to be normal. 'The weather's brightened, I see.'

'It can do as it likes,' he snapped. 'I'm not interested in the damned weather. Your conduct is my problem. You've been seen out with Templeton every night.'

She looked back at him levelly. From Jeremy this was an attack, and clearly he thought it was his duty to chastise her. She would have thought his mother would be only too glad to see the back of her. He no longer looked as he had looked. His eyes were hard and cruel. It dawned on her that she really hadn't known him at all.

'Yes, I have. I can't think what's wrong with that. It's not as if we're engaged, Jeremy.'

'I've put a lot of time in on you, Georgina,' he grated. 'I didn't do it so that you could go about making an exhibition of yourself with Templeton. That's not the image I want for a wife.'

'Really, I wasn't aware that I'd made an exhibition of myself. Steven would quite disapprove. How have I offended?'

Georgina was so intrigued that she couldn't seem to get annoyed. There was this unreal feeling that wouldn't go away, and Jeremy was adding to it by behaving quite out of character. He was red-faced again with temper, and she couldn't help thinking he would make somebody a terrible husband. All the same, she felt guilty. Years of friendship were being thrown away.

'All those fancy gowns,' he scoffed.

'You have a telescope, Jeremy? I don't remember calling round to show you my dresses.'

'Don't think your tongue's going to get you out of this one. I'm not going to stand by while you make a fool of yourself. He was never short of women but you're not going to be one of them. This can stop right now. You're my girl!'

'Gina is Steven's girl. Always was, always will be,' Celia's voice cut in coolly, as sharp as glass. She had approached with the same silence that Steven had, and she took Georgina's arm firmly.

'You keep out of this, Miss Uppity Templeton!' Jeremy was so enraged that he glared at Celia, and Georgina was quite stunned. She couldn't help thinking that his mother would not approve of this, unless she had put him up to it and was watching from the sidelines.

'How crude!' Celia looked down her aristocratic nose at him and turned Georgina away. 'Come along, Gina. Daddy's offering us tea in the members' stand.'

'Pah!' Jeremy scoffed and Celia raised cool eyebrows.

'Extraordinary! Come along, Gina.'

'Well, it's not much different from "bah",' Georgina murmured as they walked off and left him to his temper. Any urge she had felt to explain to him had gone as he had turned to Celia. She felt almost hysterical. The things that happened to her! She could feel a smile growing that was soon going to turn into laughter. She hadn't lost her temper once. Come to think of it, she hadn't lost her temper since Steven had announced that he wanted her.

Celia led her round the side of the stand, and then they both stopped and looked at each other before falling into each others' arms, shaking with laughter.

'How cruel we are,' Georgina said, wiping her eyes. 'It's not very nice.'

'It wouldn't have been very nice if Steven had caught him speaking to you like that,' Celia pointed out. 'He would have killed him. You took it calmly,' she added, looking at Georgina closely. 'Actually, I intervened before you hit him.'

Well, she didn't do things like that now, did she? Steven had tamed her.

'I should never have gone out with Jeremy,' she mused. 'I suppose I led him on a bit. Now he's upset.'

'Oh, rubbish! He'll tell his mother and they'll both get hours of pleasure pulling you to pieces. Let's get our tea while it's still on offer.'

She was out in the village the next day when Steven came home, and she didn't see him arrive. All day she had hardly been able to do anything. She had started to get ready immediately after lunch, ignoring work and calling herself all manner of a fool. She had new jeans on, and a lovely green sweater that had cost the earth. Steven liked her in green, though, and she was so excited that nothing made any impression on her.

When she got back home it was almost time for him to arrive, or so she thought until Celia rang.

'I just wanted to remind you it's the ball this weekend,' she said, 'We've got to get it organised. Mummy wants to know if you're in for your usual stint?'

'Of course I am. I'll come up in the morning for the discussion. When Steven gets here we're going out.'

'But he's here already. I thought you knew. He's been here for about two hours.'

Something in Georgina went cold. He hadn't rung her, hadn't come down to see her. After London he had changed his mind. She heard his voice then—clearly he had come to the phone and dispatched Celia.

'Is—is anything wrong?' She could hear her own voice trembling and she started to tremble too when he answered.

'What could be wrong? I'm back.' She knew that sardonic way he had of speaking and her heart fell even more.

'I didn't expect you to arrive until about now.'

'I managed to get off early. If you're ready I'll be down to collect you in about fifteen minutes.' He just put the phone down and there was no seductive murmur, no warmth.

She stood looking at the phone blankly for a minute and then rushed to tidy her hair. As far as she could see, she was ready. He had said not to dress up and she had gone as far as she could to be glamorous in jeans. Something was wrong and she could only think he had decided to forget all about wanting her. He would tell her tonight, she just knew he would. He might even tell her he was going to marry Auriel. Maybe he had come back early to tell Malcolm? She started to tremble as if she would never stop.

Georgina did what she always did when she was agitated. She went round to speak to Stardust. Just looking at Stardust calmed her, and she almost ran round to the loose-box, wanting as many minutes as she could get before Steven arrived. When he told her she would have to face it calmly. There would be no tears.

She flung the doors open and then stopped in great shock. The loose-box was completely empty. Stardust was gone.

For a second she just stood looking at the empty space, and then she raced back round to the house, intent on phoning the police. It wasn't that Stardust was a valuable horse, although she was very well bred. If there were horse thieves around then they would surely have hit the stables at Kellerdale Hall first. Royal was worth a small fortune. Who would have bypassed him to get to Stardust? How had they got her off the estate?

As she raced round into the drive Steven drew up, the sleek car looking somehow menacing. And that was exactly how he looked. He unfolded himself from the driving seat and just stood watching her. He could see what a state she was in but he made no move to come quickly towards her, and it was Georgina who had to go to him.

'Stardust is missing!' She went across and told him in an agitated voice, almost jumping about with anxiety.

All he did was walk round to her and open the passenger door.

'Get in,' he said coldly.

'Didn't you hear what I said? Stardust is missing. Look! It's getting dark. I've got to do something now!'

'Stardust is not missing,' he stated with cool firmness, his icy looks not at all fading. 'Stardust is back home, in the stables.'

He thrust her inside the car and came round to get into the driving seat.

'What do you mean?'

For the first time in many days she felt the flicker of her old temper. He seemed pretty sure that Stardust was safe, and there was no way she could have got out alone and trotted back home. It wasn't home anyway.

'How did she get there?' Georgina demanded as he simply started the engine and moved off down the drive.

'I came home early, as you now know,' he said flatly. 'Naturally I came to see you but you were out. I heard a very horsy noise and went to investigate. Imagine my surprise to find Stardust locked in her little hole and not comfortably at the hall as I'd expected.'

'I decided to keep her here,' Georgina said, fighting down anxiety. He was very angry, she could see that.

'And neglected to tell me. Not one word in all the days we've been together. Not one little whisper in my ear. You don't change much, do you, Georgina?' he added grimly. 'You'll fight me to the last breath, even if you have to do it surreptitiously.'

'I'm not surreptitious!' She didn't know whether to feel guilty or furious. It had given her a very nasty shock to find Stardust gone, but he wasn't bothered about that. All that concerned him was that she had defied him a little. It was only a little, she told herself, and anyone other than a domineering male would have laughed about it.

'I can keep Stardust at home if I want to,' she said defiantly. 'I have rights, you know.'

'Yes,' he growled. 'You have rights. Perhaps I might have been inclined to be amused and indulge you as usual, knowing your childish ability to defy, but when I took Stardust out my eye fell on another door, an open door, and inside what do you think I saw? A newly repaired, gleaming motorbike.' He flashed her a look of such anger, such contempt, that she quaked.

'I haven't ridden it,' she began, and then felt furious with herself at this meek manner. What a crime! She had kept her own horse and had her own motorbike repaired. It was heinous, obviously. What about Steven's crimes? He had left her and gone down to London to Auriel. He intended to seduce her and then go back to Auriel again.

'You haven't ridden it—yet,' he corrected icily, 'nor will you get the chance. I've removed it too.'

'It's *mine*!' Her temper roared like an open furnace door, the old Georgina back with a vengeance, and she turned flashing eyes on him, her gleaming hair swinging round her furious face. 'You have no right to interfere with my belongings. It has nothing to do with you whatever.'

'Hasn't it?' he enquired grimly, his own temper prowling like an angry tiger. 'I'm not about to sit by with a docile smile until you've killed yourself.'

'If I choose to kill myself it's my affair!'

'No, it isn't. You're mine.'

'Not yet, I'm not,' she cried bitterly, 'and you can wipe that completely out of your mind. After this I can see Jeremy's good points. *And* I'm leaving Kellerdale! Let me out!'

CHAPTER EIGHT

GEORGINA made a grab for the door catch, her temper blinding her to danger, and Steven's hand left the wheel as he caught hold of her arm.

'Stop that!' It was the only thing he had time to say, because she lashed out at him with her arm, striking his hand away and knocking the steering-wheel. It spun in his hands and before he could right the car it had turned wildly towards the deep ditch at the side of the road, pitching forward and into it nose first.

Before they crashed Steven flung himself forward, his body across her, protecting her, and then there was a terrible noise as the car dived headlong and Steven's head crashed into the windscreen.

It had happened so suddenly that it was almost unreal. He gave a low groan and then fell sideways, blood pouring down his face, and Georgina scrambled across to him, tearing off her seatbelt and reaching for him.

'Steven! Steven! Oh, Steven!'

He was out cold and she didn't know what to do. She was utterly distraught, holding his hand and gazing pitifully at him. Why didn't people just come when you wanted help? They were always there when they were not wanted. She was moaning his name like a lost soul and he stirred, opening dazed eyes and looking up at her, his powerful body collapsed against the door, the whole car at a crazy angle.

'I'll live, George,' he assured her huskily, clearly very dazed indeed. 'Help me out of this damned car and up to the hall.'

'Our house is nearer,' she said anxiously, her hands making desperate little movements against his face. 'I'll phone the doctor. I'll phone your mother. I'll——'

'Just move back and let me out,' he suggested wryly, the back of his hand wiping at the blood. 'We'll decide what panic-stricken action to take then.'

'You're bleeding!' she wailed. 'I almost killed you.'

'Nothing in this world is ever really new,' he joked groggily. 'You've been killing me for years. Now let's get out of here.'

She crawled out, backing all the way. Her door was on top and Steven had to make a major effort to struggle free. He looked terrible and, to cap everything off, it started to rain again.

Tears were streaming down Georgina's face, mixing with the rain, and she valiantly put her arm round him, urging him to lean on her. He was evidently shakily amused.

'If I do we'll both fall over. Just hold my hand, George, and let's get out of this damned rain.'

He was calling her George and she had never been so glad in her life about anything, because she had thought for one terrible moment that she would never hear his wonderful voice again. Right now he could have called her anything and she would have been thrilled to hear it.

She got him up to the Dower House and into the drawing-room. The fire was still going, the whole room nicely warm, and he sank down on to the settee, looking pale and shocked. Georgina bit her lip anxiously and then ran out and grabbed a towel from the kitchen, coming back to make desperate little dabs at his forehead where the blood was now slowly drying.

'I'll just see to you, then I'll phone the doctor,' she murmured seriously, her eyes intent on her task. Her father was still at the show with Sir Graham. They wouldn't be back yet. All this would upset Lady Evelyn terribly. She adored Steven. Everyone did, but no one as much as herself.

He put out a hand and held her wrist, smiling at her wryly.

'Just make me some tea, Georgie. I'm slowly recovering. No need for the doctor.'

'You made me have the doctor when I skidded. You look awful.'

'It's just a bump. Nothing to worry about.'

'But you're so pale!'

She knelt in front of him and suddenly couldn't bear it. If anything happened to Steven... She brushed the thick black hair from his forehead while he watched her with amused eyes, and she gasped at the size of the bruise there. It was already turning colour, blood all around it, and she was anguished.

'Oh, Steven!' She put her arms around him, wanting to rock him and hold him, protect him as he had always protected her. He wouldn't be like this if he hadn't flung himself in front of her. Tears streamed down her face and she held him closer, pulling him into her arms. 'Steven,' she wept.

She overbalanced them both, and he slowly fell forward, not enough strength left to save either of them. Georgina landed on the thick carpet with Steven halfway over her, and she was still trying to save him, her arms tightly round him.

He looked down at her, amusement in his blue eyes, although his colour was still pale.

'I'm no match for your fiery strength at this moment,' he said quietly. 'We seem to be where we started, in a state of collapse.'

'I'm sorry. Please don't tease, Steven. You're too ill.'

'Honestly, I'm not.'

She searched his face anxiously. He seemed to be recovering by the minute. Maybe it was because he was lying down? He raised himself up on one elbow and looked down into her distressed face.

'I'm all right,' he said quietly. 'I'm not going to end up as a body on the rug.'

'Don't! Don't joke about it. It was all my fault. I've hurt you badly with my awful temper and my irritating ways.'

'Not an awful temper,' he corrected softly, 'just colourful, and I'm not badly hurt at all.' He wiped her tears and she could only look at him, neither of them attempting to move. Each time he went away everything seemed to stop, the days empty.

Her lovely eyes searched his face. Why had she thought he was treacherous? What had he really done? It was merely her desire to cling to him, a desire that had always been there from a child's affectionate fixation to a woman's passionate love. He had gone to look after the family interests, gone to live in Canada and then London, and why not? She had not been a woman, she was only that now. She had not been able to forgive him, to remember his past kindness. Which one of them was treacherous?

Tears filled her eyes again and she turned away, blinking rapidly to clear them, but his lean hand turned her back to face him.

'You're crying again. What's hurting you, Georgina?'

'Nothing,' she whispered. 'I didn't want you to be dead.'

'I'm not.' He bent his head and kissed her eyes closed, and just as she was thinking she had better call for help, get the doctor, or at the very least someone from the hall, his lips closed over hers.

'Don't move. Don't move away from me,' he said huskily. 'I need you here.'

Almost protectively her arms moved round his neck, clinging to him, but he needed no protection. His body was suddenly full of vibrant life, every powerful muscle taut, and he moved right over her, crushing her, kissing her until she melted against him, pliant and soft.

'I dream of this,' he murmured thickly. 'Looking down and seeing your face, feeling you beneath me.'

She could feel the weight of his body, feel it harden against hers, and a wonderful lethargy softened her more. There was the crackle of the fire, their unsteady breathing and nothing else in the world. Neither of them thought of anyone coming in. Georgina was molten in his arms and his desire was already raging, almost beyond control.

His hand slid beneath her sweater to close around her breast, and he murmured with pleasure.

'Silky and soft, warm as a kitten.' With one swift movement he pulled the sweater over her head, looking down at her, his eyes almost on fire. 'What I've dreamed of for years.' His head bent to nuzzle against her. 'You worry about me, Georgina? It's worth the bump on the head.' He took one rosy nipple in his mouth and she arched against him, frantic with desire, gasping and moaning, her bright head tossing from side to side, her whole body trembling.

'Do you want me?' He clasped her head, holding it still, and he didn't really have to ask. Her eyes and her trembling, aching body told him.

'Do you?' he insisted softly, his breathing harsh and unsteady.

'Yes, oh, yes!'

'Then come to me, Georgina. I want you so badly. I ache for you.'

She pressed herself against him, eager to be closer, and felt the surge of masculine triumph race over his body. Both of them seemed to be going up in flames and she began to spin away, whispering his name as he kissed her, caressed her, his hands urgent. It was now. In a minute she would belong to Steven and nothing else mattered.

'Steven! Steven!' She sobbed his name, clinging to him, and his breath mingled with her own.

'Do you love me?' he demanded, almost cruel in his desire. 'Do you love me, Georgina?'

'Yes, I love you. I've always loved you. I can't live if you're not there.'

'Georgina! Georgina!' He gasped her name, arching her against him, his face between her breasts, and then suddenly she knew he was different. He was more heavy, as if he didn't care about hurting her. His lips were lifeless and his hand fell away.

In a wild panic she opened her eyes, and when she touched him he rolled away, his eyes closed, a deadly pallor beneath his tan.

'Georgina.' He just murmured her name and then he was perfectly still, unconscious.

She wanted to scream but she wriggled free, kneeling over him, rubbing his hands, terrified. He didn't move and she placed her head against his chest, listening for his heart, almost missing it because her own heart was beating erratically. It was there, the strong, steady beat she knew so well. She had to get help!

She scrambled across to the telephone, not bothering to dress, frantically pushing buttons, and it was Steven's father who answered.

'Come! Oh, come quickly! Get a doctor. He's hurt.'

'Georgina!' Sir Graham's voice pulled her up, restored some measure of sanity. 'Calmly, slowly, tell me what it is.'

She managed to tell him, taking deep breaths to calm herself. And when he knew about the accident and how Steven was now unconscious he went swiftly into action.

'We'll be there in two minutes. Bill Davis is here now. He came back with your father and me. Calm down, Georgina.'

By the time they arrived she was dressed properly, kneeling by Steven, her face paper-white, but she knew what she had to say.

'I managed to help him back here but he said he was all right. I was going to make him a cup of tea and he collapsed.'

Somehow, once again, she felt it was all her fault, and her tragic face showed it.

They decided to keep him in hospital overnight. The X-rays had cleared any worries but he was concussed and decidedly groggy, and in spite of his protests he was kept in until morning.

'And then a few days in bed, whether he likes it or not,' Bill Davis said as he came out to the waiting-room to tell them.

'Can I go in?' Georgina asked quickly, but he was adamant.

'Definitely not. You've had a bad shock yourself. I've told you he's all right. It's bed for you too. Get her home, Harry. I'll give you a couple of sleeping pills for her.'

She wanted to insist but she could see that the three men with her would not stand for it. And his father would be going in to him. She wasn't really anything in Steven's life after all. Their desire for each other was a dark secret, something that would hurt everyone if they knew.

She went with her father but she was very silent, worrying and thinking. In the ambulance Steven had come round, looking surprised to see her there, sitting by him and holding his hand.

'Hello, Sunflower. What are you doing here?' he had asked after looking at her for a minute.

It had scared her. He'd been looking at her as if he remembered nothing at all and she wondered if he had serious head injuries.

'You had an accident,' she'd reminded him urgently. 'You banged your head.'

'Oh, yes. Now I remember,' he'd said softly. 'You lost your temper again.' He had then just closed his eyes, patting her hand. Didn't he remember anything else? Didn't he remember what had happened at the house? She worried about it all the way home and her father looked at her gravely and insisted that she take the sleeping pills. She didn't protest. She was back to unreality, almost believing she had dreamed it all.

Steven was allowed home the next afternoon. He was brought by ambulance, to his great disgust, and the doctor foiled him by giving him a strong sedative as soon as he was in bed. It kept him inactive, as Bill Davis said with satisfaction.

'You can't ignore concussion,' he pointed out to Sir Graham. 'He needs another two days in bed. You never can be sure what will happen after a blow to the head.'

Georgina had gone up to the hall to start helping with the arrangements for the Easter ball and she had listened, wide-eyed. Steven had already been brought back when she had arrived and she couldn't beg to go to him. Perhaps they would indulge her and allow her to creep up to his room, but it might make them think a little.

She found herself avoiding their eyes. If they knew what Steven had planned, what so very nearly had happened... It kept her on edge the whole day, and every time she tentatively asked how he was she was told he was sleeping.

Everybody was gloomy without Steven, and Auriel was behaving as if she were Steven's fiancée rather than Malcolm's. She briskly set about tasks for the ball, doing everything wrong, driving Steven's mother into a dither and saying 'Shh!' when anyone spoke, as if Steven would be disturbed in this great house.

'Thank goodness this day is over,' Celia muttered at teatime. 'I'll walk back some of the way with you, Gina.'

'Nothing is going right,' she complained as they walked down the drive. 'We all know exactly what to do. Heavens, haven't we done it for years? Mummy is giving Auriel little tasks to make her feel part of things, but she's interfered with my efforts all day—yours too. She even went in to have a word with Cook. Mummy had to do some placating there.' She gave a sigh. 'And then there's Steven.'

'It was all my fault,' Georgina said miserably. 'We were having an argument. I lost my temper.'

'Well, everybody has little fights,' Celia soothed, tucking Georgina's arm in hers.

'I knocked the wheel. He got hurt saving me. He just flung himself across me and now look where he is.' She started to cry softly and Celia squeezed her arm.

'You love him a lot, don't you? Don't worry, he'll be all right.'

It wasn't that. Georgina knew he would be all right. He was strong and powerful. The tears were partly for herself. Today had shown her that she didn't really belong. All she had ever been was a favoured subject after all. The Templetons went on their own commanding way. She could never match Steven, even if her dreams came true and he married her.

Next day Georgina arrived at the hall to find Lady Evelyn on the edge of temper for the first time in her life.

'I want you to go up to Steven and talk him to pieces,' she stated as soon as she saw Georgina. 'He's being impossible. He intends to get up straight after lunch and nothing will deter him. I'm run off my feet with the arrangements and I'm busy stopping all telephone calls to

Steven. If he gets a call from London he'll be up and away, and he's just not well enough.'

'You—you want me to go up to his room?' Georgina asked, feeling stunned.

'I most certainly do. You're the only one who can keep him entertained. Run along, dear. It's the last room on the corridor overlooking the park. You know the house well enough.'

She did, but she had never been in Steven's room before. It was like a step in the dark and she went up rather anxiously. Yesterday she had known it would be wrong to ask. Now she was almost being ordered up there.

She was a bit scared of facing Steven too, even though she was dying to see him. She didn't know if he would be angry now, and she was worried about the way she had told him she loved him. She had vowed to keep that to herself, some little shield against him.

When she gave a timid tap on his door he just snapped out, 'Come in!' and it wasn't at all encouraging. She went in, though, and just stood in the doorway, feeling like an intruder.

As soon as he saw her the exasperation left his face and he said nothing at all, just looking at her steadily. She was in a dark blue dress, her hair like fire in the sun that came in a shaft of light and caught her like a spotlight as she stood worriedly just inside the room.

Apparently he was just going to stare at her, and she moved nervously.

'Your mother asked me to come up and—and talk to you.'

'Ah! She played her trump card, did she? That was cunning. What are you supposed to do—keep me prisoner?'

'I have to talk you to pieces,' Georgina said seriously and he laughed, his brilliant eyes flashing like blue flames.

'Come and do it, then. I'm bored to tears.' He patted the bed right beside him and she moved nervously forward, hesitating. He was sitting propped up with pillows, black silk pyjamas looking elegantly severe against the white. He seemed to be better and she could see he was fretting to be up.

'You can sit down,' he murmured sardonically when she just stood looking at him. 'I'll curb my fierce instinct to drag you into bed with me.'

She blushed softly and hastily got a chair, putting it by the bed and folding her hands demurely in her lap. If she pretended it was like visiting him in hospital it would be all right.

'You've got a big bruise,' she offered seriously, looking at his head and avoiding his derisive eyes.

'It's not bad,' he agreed, giving her an ironic look. 'Is that stage one of plan B? Tell me I look terrible?'

'You don't, as a matter of fact,' Georgina said, perking up a bit. 'And it was just conversation.'

'Very good. What's next?'

'If you're going to be like this then I'll go,' Georgina snapped, standing and pushing the chair back.

His hand shot out and grasped her wrist, giving a quick tug that brought her towards him with a rush.

'If you do I'll get up and ride Royal,' he threatened. 'Sit close to me, Georgie. I want to hold your hand.' She was sitting on the bed, her hand in his before she could catch a breath, and he smiled up at her. 'Now you can talk.'

'I—I don't know what to say now.'

'Bedrooms frighten you?' he asked softly. He relented when she looked as if she wanted to run. 'Are you all right? You weren't injured in the crash?'

'No. Just scared. I nearly killed you with my temper.'

'You didn't,' he assured her seriously. 'Don't go burdening your conscience with that. You must have been quick with the ambulance.'

'I phoned when we got back to the house,' she reminded him, going quite still inside. 'You said you didn't need a doctor but then you collapsed.' She was flushed and agitated, remembering how he had collapsed, and he looked at her with a slight frown.

'When "we" got to the house? We came back here?'

'No, the Dower House. I helped you back.'

He looked at her steadily and then gave a rueful laugh.

'What a damned thing. I seem to have lost a bit of time somewhere.'

She didn't know whether to be glad or sorry. He didn't remember anything about making love to her, about her saying she loved him. No wonder he had looked surprised to find her beside him in the ambulance.

'You—you remember the accident?'

'Of course. I thought I remembered everything. What a shock.'

'So you should do as Bill Davis says and stay in bed,' she assured him speedily.

'Are you sure you're not inventing the trip to the Dower House to convince me to stay here?' he asked, his lips quirking, and she shook her head vigorously.

'No, Steven. It's all true.'

'Have I forgotten anything else?' he asked softly. 'I haven't hallucinated that you've dropped Ripley and started going out with me, have I?'

'No.' She looked down, avoiding his intent eyes, and he tilted her face up, his gaze running over her.

'I'm glad about that, then. I was scared I was having erotic dreams.' He pulled her forward, his hand clasping her nape, his lips brushing over hers. 'Mother knows how to cope with me,' he murmured seductively. 'I'd stay in this bed a lot longer if you slid in beside me.'

She just had time to gasp his name in trembling shock when his lips captured hers and he pulled her into his arms, kissing her hungrily.

'Oh, Georgie, I needed that,' he said huskily as he let her go. 'It's time you belonged to me. Just as soon as I get out of this damned bed.'

She was utterly bewildered. He was just stepping back in time. He hadn't even mentioned her motorbike or Stardust. No remonstrations. Just this determination to make her his mistress. She was flushed and breathless, just looking at him, when there was a knock on the door and Steven frowned in exasperation.

'Obviously we need a secret place of our own,' he muttered, making her feel wicked and a dangerous woman. 'Come in!' he finished sharply.

It was Auriel, and when she saw Georgina sitting on the bed she looked as if she was going to scream with rage.

'Isn't this taking things too far, Steven?' she asked angrily. 'Now that girl is up here in your room.'

From bewilderment and shock to wickedness and blushes, Georgina exploded into rage.

'Which girl are you talking about exactly?' she demanded. She was jumping up, ready to go into furious action, but Steven grabbed her wildly moving hands, pulling her back, his eyes like blue ice on Auriel.

'Here I was, worrying about a tiny loss of memory,' he said coldly. 'Your memory seems to be troubling you too, Auriel. You're Malcolm's finacée and this is *my* room. As to Georgina, I thought we'd already made our relationship quite clear to you once—another loss of memory apparently.'

'Funny, I never heard you mention her when we were in London,' Auriel said bitterly. 'You know how I felt about you,' she continued as if Georgina weren't there at all.

'Very strongly,' Steven said sardonically. 'You were so attached to me that you became engaged to my brother. I call that real devotion.'

Auriel turned and marched out, two spots of high colour on her cheeks, and Georgina subsided to the chair, her face quite pale.

'Don't let her upset you, Georgina,' he said quietly. 'She's not our problem.'

'No, she's Malcolm's problem,' Georgina managed quietly. 'She's going to marry him when it's you she wants.'

He couldn't stop her as she walked out of the room. There was little point in staying, after all. Hadn't she just been there listening to a lovers' quarrel? Outside in the corridor, Georgina leaned against the wall, tears slowly forcing their way beneath her tightly closed lashes. She stood for a second as they trickled down her cheeks and then she moved to the back stairs, running down them and making her way to the courtyard at the back of the hall, grateful that she knew this house as if it were home. It never would be again. Her suspicions were confirmed, from Steven's own lips.

When Celia rang the next morning she told Georgina that Steven had got up and gone to London, in spite of his accident. All she had to do now was wait for Auriel to join him. She felt as if she hadn't a bit of life left in her.

There was only one thing that got her through the next few days. Rowena arrived. The one good thing that had come out of boarding-school was Rowena, the original nut-brown maiden. The whole thing would have been an unbearable misery without her. Two years younger than Celia and therefore not in the same year, Georgina had expected to be utterly lonely; away from her beloved Kellerdale, away from her adored Steven, she had seen nothing but unhappiness stretching ahead, but Rowena had arrived on the same day, equally rebellious but ready for anything.

Miraculously she was here now, just when life was at its blackest. A crazy little sports car drew up outside the Dower House and Rowena stepped out, her brown eyes flashing a look of pleasure at the scene before she ran forward and almost bowled Georgina off her feet in a great hug.

'I'm here! Lead me to the Easter ball!'

'But I—I don't understand——'

'Celia invited me and I'm to stay with you here. I thought I'd keep it to the surprise that Celia wanted.'

Celia didn't deal in surprises. Shocks were more in her line, but Georgina had never been so glad to see her friend. Curly brown hair, brown eyes, pink cheeks—there was something so *wholesome* about Rowena that troubles seemed to fade away.

'I've got the most fabulous dress for this ball,' Rowena announced excitedly. 'It's orange!'

Georgina didn't know whether to laugh or cry. One thing she did know from past experience: she was going to be kept very busy with Rowena. Rowena never stopped talking.

All evening she kept both Georgina and her father entertained and it was only when bedtime came around that anything serious was mentioned.

'How is the fabulous Steven?' Rowena asked, sitting on Georgina's bed and kicking her shoes off.

'He's in London.'

Georgina hung her head and then began to brush her hair vigorously. Rowena had spent many nights listening about Steven as Georgina talked her misery away at school. Things were different now, though. It was no longer a schoolgirl crush to be talked through.

Rowena came and knelt beside her, looking up into her face.

'You've never changed, have you? It's still Steven. How does he feel about you? He always cared about you, Gina. He was there at school every open day, every prize-giving. Remember how he used to take us out for cream teas? I could have fallen for him myself if I hadn't known he was your hero.'

'There's a woman,' Georgina said unhappily. 'It's been going on for a long time. I think he might finally m-marry her.' She burst into tears and Rowena stood and put her arms around her.

'Oh, Gina! I'm so sorry. What can I do? I'll do anything.'

'Just back me up. Get me out of there if you have to. Don't let me make a fool of myself.'

'As if you would.'

'Oh, I would,' Georgina stated miserably, looking up with tear-drenched eyes. 'When Steven marries I'll have to leave Kellerdale. I'll have to leave before then. I just couldn't bear it if. . .'

She was hushed and hugged but it made no difference. She could no more tell Rowena than she could tell Celia. How could you tell anyone that the love of your whole life simply wanted you for a while? How could you say that he wanted his brother's fiancée? They would be shocked at Steven, and who would be the traitor then?

It was true that she had thrown herself at him her whole life long, almost begging for what he now wanted. Could she blame him? He was a man, after all. And he did care about her in his own way. He had risked injury to himself to spare her.

She found herself telling Rowena this, everything except Steven's desire. It all came out—the motorbike,

Jeremy and his mother, the car accident, and Rowena simply listened, letting her almost babble on.

'Are you sure there's a woman in London?' she asked finally. 'He seems to spend every minute guarding you.'

'I don't want *guarding*.' Georgina almost shouted. 'I want him to love me and you can't make that happen. Anyway,' she added more quietly, 'he went away to her when I was eighteen. I don't know what went wrong between them. I never knew who it was until now.' She wasn't going to voice her suspicions, her certainty, but she had to warn Rowena about one thing. 'Malcolm's engaged,' she added, right out of nowhere.

'Really? I always thought he was lovely, so much more gentle than Steven.'

Steven could be gentle. He could touch her so tenderly and make her heart almost stop. He could hold her in arms like iron and make them feel like velvet. He could kiss her until she left the whole world behind.

'Steven can't afford to be so gentle,' Georgina said fiercely. 'He's never been able to just be himself. He's the oldest and one day he'll be responsible for everything.'

'I'm glad I'm not in love like that,' Rowena said softly with a penetrating look at her.

'I'm glad too. As to Malcolm and his problems, keep out of it, Rowena. I don't want you to be at the receiving end of Auriel's spite.'

'Is that her name? Honestly? It must be made up. Nobody is called that.'

Oh, shades of Celia! Georgina didn't know who she would have to watch at the ball. If Celia and Rowena got their heads together there would be big trouble. Nowadays she felt like everybody's old aunt. Steven had told her to grow up when she was eighteen and crying in his arms. Well, it had taken a bit of time but she had finally made it. There was now no inclination to fight, scratch or kick. She was Miss Georgina Summers, watching her friends with reproving eyes, keeping them out of mischief. What had happened to George?

Georgina's hands were actually shaking as she got ready for the ball. Steven would be there and, whatever happened, nothing must give her away, not by even one look must she show how much she was hurting. She carefully put on eye-shadow and darkened her lashes even more, looking critically at her hair in the mirror. Unlike the rest of her, it was glowing, dark and light, and tonight she had it swept up behind her head, falling in soft waves to her shoulders. It added to the delicacy of her appearance and she realised there was not a trace of colour in her face.

She slid her dress over her head and adjusted it before looking at herself again. It was not green. She couldn't wear green, not for Steven, not tonight. The dress was a soft pale lilac, drifting chiffon swept back over a satin shift of the same colour. Her creamy shoulders were bare and she fastened her necklace carefully. Her fingers were trembling so much that she took a long time to get it fixed, and she was just dabbing on perfume when Rowena came into her room.

'Oh, Georgina. You're quite beautiful,' Rowena said softly. 'You look almost unreal.' She came forward quickly and gave Georgina an unexpected kiss on her cheek. 'Why don't you just back out of this? Obviously it's torture to you.'

'Do I look that bad?'

'You look just about perfect but I know what this is costing you.'

'I can't back out,' Georgina said firmly, turning to the mirror. 'I've never backed out of anything in my life.'

'Then I'm right with you,' Rowena assured her. 'What do you think of my orange dress?'

Whatever it was, it was not orange, Georgina decided. As Rowena moved the colours changed from a creamy orange tint to a soft brown, and it suited Rowena to perfection. Nothing, though, could remove that look of sheer good nature. The brown curly hair was secured high on her head and escaped in small ringlets behind her ears. From her brown eyes to her dimpled cheeks she looked healthy, merry and wickedly wise.

'You look gorgeous, girl,' Georgina said with a smile, and Rowena gave her a very straight look.

'Good!' she said firmly. 'I plan to knock 'em sideways.'

Who? Malcolm? The family? Georgina's inner quakings came back instantly. This night would be very, very difficult.

Her father was very impressed, called them luscious beauties and led them off to the hall with a great deal of pride. Georgina had never needed him as much in her whole life and she clung to him so tightly as they entered the hall that he looked down and patted her hand.

'What is it, love?' he asked in a low voice. 'You're not ill?'

'I'm fine,' she lied with a smile, and Rowena took her arm firmly as Sir Graham and Lady Evelyn came out to greet them.

'I'll keep an eye on her,' she whispered.

'No need,' Harry Summers said with a smile. 'Steven is back.'

Georgina had already noticed that. He was nowhere to be seen but right at the top of the great staircase a huge black dog sat and eyed the incoming guests with interest. It was clear that Prince had been told not to take even one step down the stairs, and who could issue such orders and have them obeyed but Steven?

Almost immediately her father was involved with new guests, who were arriving by the second, and it was clear that this Easter ball was going to be every bit as successful as previous ones. Malcolm came up with Auriel, who looked splendid and aloof, quite the wrong attitude for a charity ball, and she was not at all pleased when Malcolm complimented Georgina and Rowena on their appearance.

'So many beauties tonight,' he smiled. 'One could become quite addicted.' To Georgina he was almost a brother, but his tone brought the soft colour back into Rowena's face, and as Auriel moved forward quite bossily to take her share of greeting the incoming guests, a task always left to Sir Graham and Lady Evelyn, Malcolm murmured that there were drinks if you knew where to look.

'Steve will be down any minute,' he added to Georgina, and from this she assumed that she was to stay right where she was while he had Rowena to himself. He had been like this since Rowena had arrived. He certainly seemed to be living dangerously but, as Rowena hadn't started it, Georgina felt quite justified in hanging back. Not that she was about to wait for Steven.

In fact, she felt just a little panic-stricken, a stranger in a hostile land. All around her was gaiety and laughter, the sound of the musicians already tuning up in the old ballroom, friends arriving and greeting each other, but Georgina seemed to be standing on a little island all alone, bathed in the light of the huge chandelier that glittered in the entrance hall, and she was still almost frozen in time when Steven came.

She saw him appear at the head of the stairs and immediately Prince stood up with a great deal of expectancy. He sat again quickly as Steven snapped his fingers and simply pointed. Right at that moment Georgina felt as if she would do the same. It was not in her power to move.

He saw her as he was about halfway down the stairs and he, too, stopped, his expression changing dramatically. One moment before he had been almost smiling, everything about him relaxed, but as soon as he saw her he became uncannily still and he paused, looking down at her. His hair was as black as the dinner-jacket he wore and she was utterly captured by the sapphire-blue of his eyes.

For a minute he just stood and looked at her, his face curiously taut, and she knew then what he was going to tell her. There was no longer any doubt. He might not have arranged it now but he had made his mind up. Georgina knew him too well to doubt it. Maybe that was why Malcolm felt it safe to chat Rowena up. Maybe they had all made their peace?

CHAPTER NINE

GEORGINA started to tremble again, unable to control the tremors, and Steven came down the rest of the stairs, his face still unsmiling. He was standing in front of her and she could do nothing but look up into his dynamic face.

'In the first place, you get more beautiful,' he said quietly, as if he was choosing his words very carefully. 'Secondly, I think you'd better tell me what's wrong.'

'Nothing.' She managed to just go on looking up at him, forcing back the tears that stung at the back of her eyes, but she had a great suspicion that he knew. He could see right through her. He had always had that power.

'Nothing?' He took both her hands, ignoring people who called out to him. 'You're ethereal, an illusion, some celestial being I conjured up out of my own imagination.' His hands tightened steadily and the narrowed blue eyes flared over her. 'What's the trauma, Georgina? Either you're ill or you're carrying some burden all tightly wrapped up inside.'

'I'm perfectly all right,' she said, willing her voice not to tremble too.

'Perfect you may be. All right you are not.'

'You're mistaken.' She smiled as brilliantly as she could and he stared right into her eyes for one heart-stopping second before turning away, his hand still holding one of hers.

'Very well. I'll play along with that for the moment.' He sounded cold and hard and Georgina decided to extricate her hand from his, but that got her exactly nowhere.

'Be still!' he ordered sharply. 'Until I know what's wrong you're with me.'

'I—I can't be. Rowena is here and I have to look after her.'

'Since when has Rowena needed looking after? I know she's here, as a matter of fact. I was told quite enthusiastically as I arrived home.'

That gave her a bit of worry. What was Celia up to now?

'I suppose Celia told you,' she probed carefully, but he shook his head and gave her quite a sardonic glance.

'Of course not. Malcolm told me.' His hand slid round her wrist when she tried to glide away. It tightened to a grip like steel. 'Isn't it odd that, after being away for so long, Rowena should get herself invited to this particular Easter ball? Fortuitous, would you say?'

'She came to see me,' Georgina stated bravely.

'And all she's seeing is Malcolm,' he finished sarcastically. 'Well, we didn't order any fireworks for tonight, but who knows? We may very well get some.'

She got the impression that he was counting this another plot. Maybe he thought that was why she was so pale and shaken. Well, if he did it was a good thing. It would put him off the scent. At least he hadn't told her Auriel was going back to him. He must be waiting until this ball was all over.

The band struck up as they went into the old ballroom. It was a dream of a place, never used except for some special occasion. At one end there was a minstrels' gallery, and now it was decked out with balloons and streamers. The room was long, high and very, very old. It was lit by four huge chandeliers that nowadays would have cost a small fortune, and already people were dancing.

'This place is more suited to the minuet than the modern dance,' Steven murmured as they stood and watched the circling couples.

'I know.' She had been fascinated by this place as a child. She had spent hours here, walking across the floor, dancing all by herself. Even then her hero had been beginning to take form in her mind. She glanced up at him and he was watching her closely.

'Are you going to tell me what's wrong now?' he asked very quietly.

'Why, nothing.' She gave another brilliant smile and his lips quirked in amusement.

'All right, Georgina. After all, what's the harm? If you collapse I'll simply pick you up. If you sneak off I'll follow you. Sooner or later you'll tell me anyway, so let's dance.'

His arms came round her and he swept her into the dancing, and after a while a little colour came back into her cheeks. She was not about to have to face things tonight after all. She wouldn't let him tell her either. The pain of it all she could keep inside, and when this was all over she would go away. She had been thinking about it for days and had even got as far as writing for an interview, but she hadn't had the courage to tell her father.

Even the thought of never seeing Steven again made her tighten up with anguish, and it must have transmitted itself to Steven because he held her closer and bent his dark head.

'Tell me what it is, Georgina,' he said softly against her hair.

'There's nothing.' She could feel her own heart beating like a drum, and he would probably feel it too. He must have done because his thumb began to probe erotically against her soft palm.

'There must be dozens of places in this house where I could take you,' he whispered against her ear. 'Nobody would find us. With so many people here nobody would look.'

Shivers began to run down her spine and he moved her closer until her legs were against his. He bent his head more and brushed his lips against her neck.

'I want you, Georgina. I want you in my arms when I wake up. This can't go on for much longer. Neither of us can stand it.'

She didn't answer. She couldn't, and when his eyes looked into hers she shook her head, looking quickly away.

'I don't want... I know about you and Auriel. There's no need to pretend. If you want a mistress I think you've already got a good one. In any case, I—I realised that I—can't...'

His hands tightened angrily, but she never finished because a movement in the doorway caught his eye right at that moment and he stiffened in rage.

'I'll be damned!' he muttered furiously. 'I can't believe my eyes.'

When Georgina looked across she couldn't believe her eyes either. Jeremy was there, *and* his mother. They were standing with somebody they knew, his mother talking animatedly, but Jeremy was looking round and she knew with a sinking heart that he was looking for her.

She could feel fury racing through the whole of Steven's body, all the more intense because he knew, as she knew, that he had to play the gracious host. This was a charity ball, not some private family gathering. The more people who came the better. Everybody came—they always had done.

'Is this why you don't want?' Steven looked down at her with flaring blue eyes. 'Is this why you've realised that you can't?'

'D—don't be silly, Steven. Everybody comes here. I'm sure they come every year. You just haven't noticed before.' She knew perfectly well they hadn't come before. Mrs Ripley was extremely suspicious of charities.

'There's not a lot escapes my eye,' Steven said tautly, 'and Ripley never. We both know who he's looking for. Is this the reason for the fragility, the ethereal beauty? You didn't have the courage simply to tell me?'

She couldn't stand here shouting at him. Already people were looking at them curiously, and Jeremy was trying to catch her attention. The nerve of men! Steven was treating her as if she were an unfaithful wife while all the time he had been with Auriel on every possible occasion. And Jeremy's cool cheek took her breath away. At the show he had been downright insulting to both her and to Celia. Now he was here with that look on his face. She didn't know why she bothered!

She pulled free of Steven and marched right out of the ballroom, cutting past Jeremy and ignoring him completely. She was fuming as she made it to the entrance hall, muttering to herself, her fists tightly clenched. In fact she was muttering so much that she didn't know Steven was there until he grasped her firmly and swung her into the library, closing the door with a bang.

'*Now* you'll tell me!' he rasped. 'If it's Ripley you want after all you'll stand there, look me in the face and say so!'

'I wouldn't have Jeremy if he was in a paper bag and tied up with ribbons!' Georgina raged. 'And just because you're in the baronial hall you needn't think you can throw your weight about with me!'

'Why is he here, then?' Steven grated.

'He's free to buy a ticket like everyone else. They've probably had their tickets for weeks. Catch Mrs Ripley wasting ten pounds a head. Now let me out. I'm going home and the Easter ball can take care of itself. And

while we're on the subject,' she added with furious
dignity, throwing up her glittering head, 'I've already
written for another job. I intend to resign on Monday.'

'Oh, do you?' Steven looked very dangerously quiet
and she had to hang on to her temper tightly to get her
out of everything. 'What exactly are you resigning from?
Does it include me? Our relationship?'

'We don't have a relationship,' Georgina stated with
more firmness than she felt. Her legs were beginning to
shake again for one thing. 'A few kisses? What does
that matter? Plenty of people have kissed me. I'd hardly
call it a relationship. Don't forget I know all about Auriel
and your plans. Anyway, I was p-playing you along.'
She didn't know how she managed to say that, and
Steven's eyes opened wide, almost drowning her in blue.

'Were you?' he purred softly, as sinister as a cougar.
'Then I really hand it to you. I had no idea. Let's go
back to the ball, then, old friends as ever.'

He swung the door open and she was really scared
then. She *knew* Steven. He never took things like this.
She decided to be both brave and dignified.

'Very well. We'll remain friends, but I really must go
home. This has quite upset me.'

She began to walk past him as he politely held the
door for her and her heart missed a beat as the familiar
hand came to her wrist, clamping round the slender bones
with no hope of escape.

'Come back to the ballroom first,' he said reasonably.
'After all, many people saw us go out, and we weren't
exactly laughing. We don't want the family upset, do
we?'

'No.' It was true, after all, and then there was Rowena,
who was her own guest.

'Well, then. We'll go back for a while, just to show
the flag.' He led her off towards the ballroom and his
hand moved until he was holding her own hand firmly.

When she stiffened, terribly aware of him, he simply twined his fingers with hers and smiled down at her, no trace of rage left.

'Surely we can put on a united front?' he asked quietly. 'Do we want everyone to think we've been having a fight?'

No, they didn't. She had to agree with that. She loved everyone too much to cause any distress.

'All right.' Her hand relaxed in his and for a second he tightened his fingers.

'That's my girl,' he said softly, and it almost had her crying. If only she were. If only she were Steven's girl. But it had to be forever and ever. She couldn't face anything else. She knew that now. She had known it for days and days really. She loved him too much. It was Steven or no one, and it could never be Steven.

By the time they got back the whole family had gathered to do their bit, and Steven threaded his way through the crowd towards them. He was extremely nonchalant, Georgina noticed, not showing any sign of his towering rage. His hand was warm and strong, firmly holding hers as he nodded and smiled to people who spoke to him. He wasn't stopping, though. There was a very purposeful air about him that was extremely worrying, and she reminded herself anxiously that she had never known Steven to back down from anything. He was taking this just too calmly.

She couldn't help noticing what a striking group the family made standing there. She had already begun to add Arnold to the family in her mind. Only Auriel seemed an outsider. Steven leaned across to say something to Malcolm, who raised his eyebrows but went off at once, and Georgina made a move to go to Rowena, who was chatting vigorously to Lady Evelyn.

Steven snapped her back to his side as if she were Prince on a leash. His hand tightened almost painfully

but he didn't look at her and she was powerless to protest.
Too many people were looking their way. They looked
even more curiously as the music suddenly stopped.
Malcolm was threading his way back to them and
Georgina realised that Steven had ordered him to stop
the band.

Her heart took off like a mad bird. She had no idea
why he had created this sudden silence but it had to be
some sort of a plan. Celia could plot to her heart's
content but Steven acted instantly. She couldn't even
begin to imagine what it was all about, but instinct told
her to duck. Unfortunately he still had her in a steel-like
grip and there was nowhere to run.

'I'm sorry to spoil the dancing for a moment,' he announced to the startled faces that turned towards them.
'This seemed too good an opportunity to miss, though.
It's the one time of the year when everyone who knows
us is gathered together in one place.' He turned his glittering smile on people who were now very intrigued. 'I'm
not above a bit of drama when the need arises.' He put
his free hand in his pocket and turned Georgina towards
him. 'The Easter ball seemed like a very good time for
Georgina and I to tell you that we are officially engaged.'

The ring was on her finger before she could even think,
a glowing ruby surrounded by diamonds, the whole thing
costly and extremely unusual, obviously specially de-
signed, and for a second Georgina just stared at it. Then
Celia and Rowena gave simultaneous shrieks of joy and
the whole place erupted into sound, people clapping,
laughing, the whole room buzzing with congratulations.
The band struck up with a dreamy, romantic waltz, and
then they were both hemmed in by family.

'You sly dog,' Malcolm laughed, shaking Steven's
hand. 'I had no idea why I was stopping that music.
What a thing to do! Georgina looks stunned.'

'She's swept off her feet,' Steven murmured, his arm coming round her tiny waist. 'She had no idea, had you, sweetheart?' He tightened her against him and she couldn't help thinking it was more threatening than romantic.

Everybody seemed to be kissing her and she wanted to sink into the ground because she knew it was all for some dark purpose. Her mind was racing around, trying to come up with a reason for it all, but she was too overwhelmed to think straight.

Sir Graham kissed her cheek soundly and there was no doubt about it—he was delighted.

'Well, it's been a long time coming but it had to happen, of course,' he stated happily. 'We've had some tricky times along the way.'

Celia pulled her right out of Steven's grasp and hugged her breathless.

'What did I tell you?' she whispered. 'Two down, one to go.'

Only Rowena seemed to see Georgina's rather frantic eyes, but there was nothing to say really. She was engaged to Steven and nobody knew what was bubbling under the surface.

'I never quite asked your permission, Harry,' Steven said with a grin at her father.

'That would have been an old-fashioned nonsense,' her father remarked, hugging Georgina again. 'I suppose, if the disgraceful truth was actually admitted, I handed her over to you years ago.'

'I—I'm sorry that you couldn't know first,' Georgina said a little anxiously as Lady Evelyn finally managed to get close. There was always more of the air of the very correct about Steven's mother than there ever was about Sir Graham.

'My dear! It was such a delightful way of doing things. Steven has always been very original and, in any case, it's not really a shock, you know. It was just a matter of time. You know how we feel about you, surely?'

Yes, she did. They were and always had been her family. How would they feel if they knew the full black depths of things?

'Come along,' Steven said firmly, taking her into his arms. 'We'll have the champagne when all these people have gone. Right now I think I'll dance you away on trembling legs.'

It was impossible to talk. There were too many people still interested, couples dancing by, offering their congratulations. If Georgina hadn't been so stunned she would have laughed aloud at the expression on Mrs Ripley's face. Clearly Jeremy's mother had taken this as a personal affront, although she had never liked Georgina. Jeremy was enraged and kept well clear, and the other interesting face belonged to Auriel. She had not once congratulated them and she seemed to be sheathed in ice.

Inside Georgina was becoming more frantic by the minute. Steven knew. She could feel the vibes coming from him but he said nothing at all. He held her implacably and it was quite a few minutes before she summoned up her courage to even whisper. Even then she dared not look into his eyes.

'Why did you do it?'

She was surprised he even heard her, but he did, and his answer didn't really shock her. She knew him too well.

'I want you, Georgina. This makes it official. That's what you expected to hear, isn't it?'

'I—I told you that——'

'That you couldn't, wouldn't, didn't want to? You're not too good at lying, my little wretch. If I picked you up now and took you out of here you'd be mine willingly.'

'Then, if you're so sure of yourself, why the engagement?'

'I have a family, sweetheart; surely you've noticed that? They expect things to be done in the proper manner.' He sounded cold-blooded, almost bored, and she gave a sort of stifled sob.

'Don't cry!' he warned quietly. 'If you do we'll be out of this room in no time flat, and I'm making no promises as to where we'll go.' Of course, it silenced her at once, and after a while Steven relaxed, his arms easing from the iron prison they had become. 'One day, George,' he said softly, 'when you're not quite such an idiot, I'll explain my actions to you. In the meantime you're an engaged lady and we have Jeremy right off our backs.'

She looked up at him but learned nothing. He simply looked back at her with satisfied blue eyes. Georgina couldn't think straight. She knew what the others did not know. She had evidence. He was still having an affair with Auriel and Malcolm didn't look as if he could care less. Right now he was dancing with Rowena and thoroughly enjoying himself. So what had Steven planned?

If looks were to be believed he had planned nothing. He had simply announced his engagement to the girl he loved, because he certainly acted like that. When the ball finally ended the family gathered in the drawing-room for a light supper with champagne for the toasts, and Steven gave every impression of being completely happy. If he didn't have his arm round her he was holding her hand, but Georgina could not relax at all.

She was wound up like a top, ready to spin off into panic. Her head was aching with unspoken thoughts and questions but she dared not voice one of them. Steven was dominating her, surrounding her, and no escape was possible, even into her own mind, because every time she looked up those brilliant, commanding eyes pinned her ruthlessly.

As for the family and her father, this was exactly what they had expected. To Arnold it was very romantic, and his eyes smiled into Celia's almost all the time. Rowena's bright, intelligent eyes took in far more, but after a while, when Steven sat on the settee and pulled Georgina into the curve of his shoulder, even Rowena gave up.

'I bet there are secret passages in this house,' Rowena said excitedly.

'Several,' Steven admitted. 'There's a priest hole on the main corridor upstairs, and somewhere or other there's a passage that comes out in the woods, an escape route in times of trouble.'

'Gosh!' Rowena's eyes looked like saucers, enthusiasm shining out of her face, and Malcolm found it all very amusing.

'Come here,' he laughed. 'If you can keep a secret I'll show you something.' Rowena, of course, jumped up at once and was standing right beside him when he pressed some hidden device in the old dark panelling. A long door slid open and Rowena gasped as she peered inside. Malcolm stepped through and turned to face her, his eyes laughing down at her.

'Come on. Lost your nerve?'

'Not me! I'm game for anything.' Rowena stepped through and the door slid closed. They could hear a little shriek and Malcolm laughing, and Georgina was quite intrigued out of her despair.

'I didn't know about that!' she complained.

'We didn't tell you,' Steven confessed, looking down at her and pulling her closer. 'You were always so damned inquisitive and tiny as a doll. We would have had to have the house demolished to find you, and *this* is a valuable property.'

He bent his head and kissed her, right in front of everyone, but luckily they thought it was quite natural and, in any case, they were waiting for the other two to reappear.

'My goodness! I hope Malcolm hasn't forgotten the exit,' Lady Evelyn laughed. 'We might have to send you in to rescue them, Graham.'

'They're taking their time,' Celia pointed out with a very tart look at Auriel, who seemed to have turned to stone. Her eyes were absolutely furious, and Georgina wondered if this was when the fireworks would begin.

Luckily they appeared at the other side of the room and Rowena stepped out laughing, with Malcolm right behind her, a wide grin on his face.

'I would absolutely hate to go into a dark, dirty passage,' Auriel said frostily, but Rowena grinned quite openly.

'Actually, it's spotlessly clean, apart from the odd cobweb. It has a light, too, but Malcolm didn't switch it on for ages.' She laughed up at him and he gave her a grin.

'I wanted to see if your nerve would give out. It almost did.'

'But not quite,' Rowena reminded him.

'Really, I can't see much point in a passage that merely goes round one room,' Auriel said cuttingly, not at all liking this intimacy. 'Not much chance of escape, is there, if you're going to pop out where the enemy is?'

'But there are other exits,' Celia said clearly. 'Doesn't one come out in your bedroom, Mal?'

'And one in the kitchen and the study,' Steven's mother said rapidly, looking quite flustered. It was a bit late, though. Celia's barb had struck home. Rowena's face flushed to a soft apricot and Auriel bristled with rage.

Georgina felt Steven's hand come up to encircle her nape.

'Just in case the rockets go off,' he said with a sort of quiet menace, 'did you have any hand in this?' He tilted her face and looked right into her eyes.

'No, Steven. Honestly,' she said quickly, not knowing exactly whether it was true or not. After all, Rowena was staying at the Dower House, and once a plot was running Celia lost all sense of proportion.

'Lucky for you,' he threatened, 'otherwise I might have to take drastic measures. One of those exits comes out in my bedroom too.' There was no sign of threat in his eyes, though. They were narrowed sensually and his hand began to move subtly against her skin with the usual devastating effect.

'Please, Steven,' she whispered, quite sure that everyone would see her beginning to melt towards him.

'Oh, you'll say that, my sweet,' he murmured. 'You'll be begging before too long, I promise.'

Georgina didn't quite know how the family smoothed things over. Without a word being said they acted in unison, polite, quiet good breeding stilling the thunder that was quivering in the air. Only Celia remained unrepentant, and Georgina saw Lady Evelyn's eyes looking for once quite angrily reproachful as they rested on her fair and defiant daughter. Rowena was quite subdued and Georgina could see that Malcolm was angry with Celia too, although, from his looks, she suspected he was annoyed that Rowena had been embarrassed.

She gave a shaken little sigh when it looked as if a crisis had been averted, and she heard Steven's soft laughter, almost against her ear.

'I do believe you've grown up, George. That quite worried you, didn't it? Those lovely golden eyes have stopped looking for a fight nowadays. You are, after all, quite ready to be an engaged lady.'

'When Celia starts I feel more like an old maiden aunt,' Georgina muttered.

'I promise you, the feeling won't last,' he murmured, and she had not one doubt about what he meant.

It was half-past two in the morning before they got back to the Dower House. Her father took Rowena, but as he started to collect Georgina too Steven intervened.

'Surely I'm allowed to walk my fiancée home, Harry?' he asked with a wide smile.

'I'd be disappointed if you didn't,' her father said. 'I'd begin to wonder what young people were coming to nowadays.'

Georgina could have told him. They were coming to plots and subterfuge, having mistresses and fiancées all at the same time. She couldn't run screaming to her father, though, and if she had done he would only have handed her back to Steven with a laugh and some merry quip. Nobody knew she was churning up inside with misery and anxiety and sheer disbelief.

Steven knew. By the time they set off the other two were already back at the Dower House and there was a cold, crisp April moon overhead. Out of sight of the house, Steven simply walked along beside her, and she cuddled into her wrap as if it was some small defence against him.

By the rhododendron hedge, completely secure from any inquisitive eyes, Steven stopped and turned her into his arms, looking down at her. For a minute he said nothing at all, his eyes searching her face. She was dazzled by the sapphire-blue and tears started to sting at her own eyes.

'What do I have to do to get you to trust me, Georgina?' he finally said rather heavily, as if he was utterly weary of her.

'We didn't have to get engaged. You gave me no choice.' There was a choking sob at the back of her voice and she looked away, but he curved his hand round her cheek, forcing her to face him.

'You don't want a choice,' he said quietly. 'You made your choice when you were about ten years old. It was me and always has been me. Ripley was just one of your madcap schemes to get free of your own desires.'

'You can say that but you don't know whether it's true or not,' she cried rather desperately. 'You've always been a force in my life. Maybe I resent it. Maybe I want to get free.'

'I see. You're going to run away from me?'

He looked down at her sardonically, not believing a word, quite sure of his hold on her, and her temper flared at once. He thought he could have everything. He thought he need only reach out and she would always be there. Steven had gone away, gone away for four years, and what had she done? She had been here, always the same, idiotic George who just folded completely when he touched her.

'I don't have to run away,' she said hotly. 'The first step will not be difficult. I'm getting a new job.'

'There's nowhere on this earth I wouldn't find you.' His face was set, hard, utterly implacable, and she felt desperate all over again.

'Why? Why? Why?' she raged, beating at his chest with both hands.

He caught them in one of his, his eyes blazing down at her.

'Because you're mine,' he said steadily. 'You've been mine for as long as I can remember, and now I want a good deal more than your mind. I want to hold you against me in the night, wake up and make love to you. I want to *own* you! There is no escape at all, so don't look for one. I know you don't trust me. I can read the

machinations of that odd little mind. I'm a traitor, a
rogue. So be it, because you're stuck with that.'

He sounded bitter, remorseless, and his mouth came
down on hers with no tenderness whatever, his hand
pulling her to his taut, angry body. It didn't seem to
make a lot of difference because she didn't struggle. She
just leaned against him, lost right from the first, and his
grip eased, his lips softening.

His hand traced her slender neck, fire at his finger-
tips, and she moaned against him, the cold, crisp night
forgotten.

'Steven! Steven!' It was the same little cry, on the edge
of rapture, and his hand slid, warm and possessive, beneath the cloudy chiffon to close over her breast.

'I'm not sure which one of us is mad,' he murmured
thickly, 'you for fighting me, or me for not taking you
years ago.' He kissed her until they were both breathless,
and just when she felt she would fall, never walk again,
he held her away from him, looking down at her with
glittering eyes.

'I'm not sure about the aunt bit,' he said huskily, 'but
I can promise you the days of being a maiden are just
about over. Go home, Georgina, while I can still let you.
I'll see you tomorrow.'

Somehow she made it, although she felt as if she was
simply floating. He had the power to remove every
thought from her mind. She was desperately in love with
him and she had no idea what his plans were. He
managed to make her feel wicked, abandoned, a slave.
She went into the house, not even looking round because she didn't have to look at him—he was there right
in her mind. She could still taste his lips, feel his hands
on her. When she got into the house she just drifted
across to the stairs and sat down on the bottom step,
too bewitched to move.

CHAPTER TEN

IN THE morning Georgina had a most astonishing phone call. Celia rang straight after breakfast and she was bursting with news.

'Listen! I can't be on the phone for more than a minute because if Steven catches me he'll kill me. In fact, I'm not sure whether he's going to kill me or hug me when he gets back. You never can tell with Steve.'

'What have you done?' Georgina asked with quick anxiety.

'Me? Nothing! What would I do?' It was Celia with all flags flying, and Georgina decided to be very firm, although she felt weak at the knees.

'If you've got news tell me now,' she commanded.

'That's what I'm trying to do, although I expect Steve will tell you later. I wanted to be the first, though.' Of course she would. Some plot had worked and the only plot to hand as far as Georgina could remember was the one about Malcolm. You never knew with Celia, though.

'It's Auriel,' Celia said with a rush, her voice dropping to conspiracy level. 'Such a scene this house has never known before. She screamed at Malcolm and threw his ring at him.'

'What!' Georgina didn't know what to believe. Auriel taking the initiative and cutting free was a bit hard to swallow.

'It's true! This morning we came down to a real shindig. Mummy was simply aghast. I mean, Auriel has no poise when you get down to it. She was like a fishwife and she didn't care who heard. She was just throwing her ring at Mal when we came in and shouting that she wasn't engaged to him any more.'

'Oh, dear,' Georgina said in her new role as maiden aunt. 'Was Malcolm upset?'

'Not that you'd notice. Of course, he was furious, but you'll never guess what! He walked over and threw it into the fire—a *diamond ring*! I bet he thought she might change her mind. Well, that just about did it. She exploded, and Steven had to come and take control. I thought Mummy was going to have the vapours.' Celia began to giggle furiously and Georgina had to be quite firm.

'So where is Auriel now?'

'Oh, she's gone. Steve took her to the station, luggage and all. Mal is walking in the woods to get his temper back. Daddy is reading the *Financial Times* very determinedly, and Mummy went to lie down. It's all been happening here. You should have come for breakfast.'

'Thank you, but some things I can bear to miss,' Georgina said firmly.

'I'll tell you in great detail when I see you. Must get off the phone in case Steven comes back. Gosh, was he furious! Steven can't stand scenes. By the time it was over he was looking down his nose at all of us as if we were rather nasty little children. I don't care to cross Steven so I'll ring off.'

It gave Georgina pause for thought. She sat down and assessed things. Auriel and Malcolm were now free of each other. Had that been the general idea? Celia thought she could plan, but Steven was the master at everything, he always had been. There would have to be a suitable interlude before he and Auriel got together.

No, it wouldn't do at all. The master he might be, but he loved his family and they would never accept Auriel as Steven's wife, not after all this, not when it meant breaking his engagement to her. Georgina was more puzzled than she had ever been.

And what about Steven's attitude to the family scene this morning? Celia had said he'd found it distasteful. Steven had had plenty of scenes with her. Did he really care for her after all? She dared not dwell on it. Any dashed hopes would just about finish her off. When she told Rowena her face went quite pale.

'I think I'd better go home, Gina,' she said sombrely. 'I feel it's my fault.'

'How could it be?'

'Malcolm was being very nice to me and I didn't object. I knew Auriel was annoyed and I thought it served her right. I like Malcolm a lot but I'm not happy about interfering in other people's engagements.'

'You're a very nice person,' Georgina said softly and got a rather wry grin.

'Fat lot of good it does me—no, forget that: never mention fat.'

She started to pack immediately, and Georgina watched for a minute and then made her mind up.

'I'm coming with you,' she said determinedly.

'What?' Rowena looked up in absolute horror. 'Steven will kill me.'

'He can't kill everyone,' Georgina said forcefully. 'At the moment it's Celia's turn. I want to get away. Invite me home with you, please.'

'You know you're welcome but, Gina, you're engaged!'

'I have to get away from Steven for a while,' Georgina muttered, twisting the lovely ring round on her finger. Not for anything in the world would she take it off. 'I have to think. You see, Steven wants me.'

'I'll say he does!' Rowena exclaimed, rolling her eyes. 'To see him looking at you makes my heart go pit-a-pat.'

'He's not necessarily going to marry me,' Georgina said softly, never looking up.

'You are engaged. That means engaged to be married. What sort of rubbish is this?'

'There's that—that other woman. She's still there, you know. He goes to her and I expect he'll keep on going to her.'

'Have you asked him about it?'

'Oh, no! I couldn't! I never ask him outright!' Georgina looked up in horror and Rowena's face softened.

'This thing between you and Steven is so intense. When you're in the same room together it's like an electric storm brewing. I always thought you should have been a very young bride. You tremble when he comes near you and his eyes just eat you up. Whatever are you both waiting for?'

'I have to get away—to think.'

'All right,' Rowena said with a smile. 'Pack your bag. Steven may not kill me outright and I was born to be a martyr anyway. I've always known it.'

Her father had much the same idea.

'Talk it over with Steven before you go,' he begged, but Georgina shook her head miserably.

'I can't, Dad. I just have to get away from him for a while. I need time to think.'

'You and Steven.' He shook his head ruefully. 'It's time you were married, my girl—all this tension is too much for your old dad. Go on, then.' He leaned across and kissed her cheek. 'Don't be surprised, though, when you come back if I'm looking for another job and waiting for a broken nose to heal.'

'Why is everyone scared of Steven? He's not at all violent.'

'You're too close to things to read the signs,' he said drily. 'Maybe you do need a breathing-space, but for God's sake go before Steven gets down here.'

For the moment Steven was engaged with other things. Thanks to Celia, she knew that, and Rowena too was anxious to be off and lose herself in the crowds of London. They made a wide detour to miss the station just in case Steven was on his way back. But it wasn't until they were miles down the motorway that either of them relaxed. Steven had a Porsche and they both knew it, although neither of them mentioned the thought of hot pursuit.

'I feel as if I'm taking Marie Antoinette away from the mob, at great personal risk,' Rowena confided, her eyes on the motorway traffic. 'How long do you think he'll be before he gets us? I have to pray a bit.'

'He'll probably not even bother,' Georgina said miserably. She was probably playing right into their hands doing this. Steven would come down to London and stay with Auriel and not bother to even look for her.

'So droll! Can you hear my hollow laughter? If he doesn't get here tonight it will be because he's taking the Dower House apart stone by stone. If you want to get away from Steven, my girl, you're going to have to ask for government protection and a new identity. Even then I wouldn't fancy your chances.'

He still hadn't arrived by next morning and Georgina knew her father would have made no attempt to cover her tracks.

Rowena's mother, who knew Georgina well, spent a great deal of time trying to fatten them both up, but Rowena was determined not to be fattened and Georgina couldn't eat a thing. They were both completely on edge and finally took the train into the city just to give themselves a bit of light relief.

It worked for a while. They had lunch and then went to Covent Garden to wander around. There was a vivacious South American band entertaining people, and they stood watching, listening to the pan pipes and the strumming guitars. Georgina managed to forget Steven for all of ten minutes, but all that was vanquished as they strolled out and hailed a taxi.

They were just getting in when a hard hand came to Georgina's arm, the grip tightening to steel. She looked round in a flutter of terror and met blazing sapphire eyes that threatened to annihilate her.

'This is the end of the line,' Steven said coldly. 'When I get you into a more private place I intend to strangle you.'

Georgina dared not say a word, but Rowena tried bravery.

'Oh! Hello, Steven,' she murmured a bit shamefacedly.

'Hello and goodbye, Rowena,' he said curtly. 'No doubt we'll meet again, but not today.' He looked down at Georgina icily. 'Come along,' he snapped, 'the great escape failed.'

'Look here!' The taxi driver boldly got out and faced Steven. 'This young lady is free to do as she likes.'

'She escaped,' Steven remarked pithily. 'I'm her psychiatrist.'

'It's all right,' Rowena got in quickly, noticing Steven's blazing eyes. 'They're engaged.'

'She doesn't look too happy,' the taxi driver mused suspiciously.

'It's her condition,' Steven informed him sarcastically. 'Persecution mania.'

'Euston Station, please,' Rowena said firmly, seeing the way the taxi driver's face was reddening with approaching anger. 'Gina, what about your clothes?'

Steven wasn't waiting—he simply dragged Georgina off and said not another word. Georgina was too scared to venture into sound. The Porsche was parked halfway on to the pavement with a fine disregard for signs, and he pushed her in and came round, pulling off at once.

'How—how did you——?'

'You left clues,' he told her harshly. 'Harry knew you were at Rowena's and Rowena's mother knew you were coming here eventually. I *do* know London.' Georgina sat and twisted her ring round and round, and Steven said not one more word.

She took no notice of her surroundings until they pulled into a quiet tree-lined square and the Porsche growled to a halt. There were very elegant houses all round, spring flowers edging the square under the trees, and Steven came round to help her out as they stopped.

'Where are we?' she asked nervously.

'Our destination,' he snapped. He took a key from his pocket and almost dragged her up the steps. It was a shining black door, she noticed dazedly. There was fan-shaped glass above it and the railings round the front were black, too, with gilt tips. Steven didn't stop to point out anything at all. He opened the door and simply thrust her inside, leading her across a hall and into a large and very luxurious flat.

He locked that door too and put the key into his pocket and she became a little wild-eyed, backing away.

'To sum things up,' he said tautly, 'I have the key and I could catch you before you got anywhere near the windows.'

He threw his jacket on to a chair and almost tore off his tie, unfastening the top button of his shirt, never taking those blazing eyes off her.

'Take your coat off,' he ordered coldly, and she backed off rapidly.

'Don't you touch me, Steven!' she told him hysterically.

'You silly little mouse,' he said scathingly. 'Where did you think all this schoolgirl nonsense was going to get you? You told Harry you wanted a break from me. Well, you've had a break—just over twenty-four hours.'

'I—I have to think…' she began anxiously, quite scared by his cold rage.

'Then do it fast,' he advised menacingly. 'You've got about two seconds.'

Somehow she had to bring calm to the atmosphere. Her common sense told her that. She had never seen Steven in quite this mood before and defiance wasn't at all advisable. She shrugged and moved with as much nonchalance as she could summon up. Unfastening her coat and taking it off took a bit of time, and all the while he watched her like a hawk, his blue eyes still blazing at her.

'If you want to talk——' she began coolly, and he simply exploded.

'Talk! I've been talking to you for years and nothing came of it but madness. Action is my plan now.'

She didn't know if he was going to make love to her or beat her but she knew she had never been so scared in her life. Steven just didn't scare her. He never had done. It was either loving or hating, but she was afraid now. She made a quick lunge and raced out of the room, through the first door she saw.

Maybe she could lock herself in until he calmed down? Unfortunately it was the bedroom, and she turned desperately to see him right behind her, leaning against the door, a cool, twisted smile on his lips.

'A step in the right direction,' he said softly, walking towards her.

'Steven! Oh, please, Steven!' She backed away and he followed relentlessly, his eyes gleaming.

'Why, I just knew you'd say that to me again,' he murmured tauntingly. 'And we're in exactly the right place for it.'

He reached for her and she knew for sure she was going to faint—her heart was going wild. She gave a soft, scared little cry and he pulled her into his arms, and then he was cradling her head against his chest, rocking her gently. She couldn't quite believe it but it had to be true. His hand was stroking through her hair.

He lifted his head and looked down at her and she couldn't believe how he was smiling either, his blue eyes dancing with amusement.

'My poor, silly baby,' he whispered. 'You still don't know where you belong, do you?'

'Steven?' She just looked back at him in a daze, and his finger gently traced her cheek.

'You're wearing my ring. Doesn't it give you any sort of security? Do we have to go on hiding behind temper and incredible, lunatic actions?'

'I—I can't be your mistress, Steven,' she whispered miserably. 'I thought I could but—but I just can't.'

'Pardon me, Miss Summers, but I don't remember asking you,' he said severely.

'You—you said you wanted me. You said it would be soon. You didn't want marriage.'

He looked at her intently for a second.

'Nothing is that simple with you, Georgina. A straightforward declaration of honourable intentions would have got just as much suspicion as anything else. The fact is you haven't trusted me for one second since you were eighteen years old, and maybe I deserved it— in a way. I remember what I said and you were devastated, I know that.' He cupped her face in strong hands and looked deeply into her eyes. 'I want you, I need you. You're going to marry me, and since last night you've been mine, officially.'

'And what about Auriel?' she said bitterly. 'You've been down here with her. You even came down when you were ill after the accident and should have been in bed. You were probably right in this room.'

She looked round with dismay and then made a blind rush for the door, but he grasped her wrist and swung her back to him, a very dangerous light in his eyes.

'You think I've been here with Malcolm's fiancée? Is that the sort of person you think I am?' He could see the truth of it in her eyes and he let her go abruptly.

'Thank you, Georgina. You've learned a lot about me over the years. I can see you admire me enormously.' He turned away and she just stood there, almost wringing her hands.

'You—you knew her before,' she began desperately. 'She's chased you since you came home.'

'Yes, I knew her!' He swung round at her savagely. 'I knew her for a few brief weeks in London before I went to Canada. We went out together a few times and she was very interested in the family estates and the title. I made one tactical error. I mentioned in her hearing that Malcolm would be coming to take my place until Arnold took over. She was cruising the waters like a shark, waiting for him.'

'And—and you were jealous,' Georgina said through trembling lips.

'Jealous? I never even kissed her hand.' He turned away in disgust. 'What do you need with me, Georgina? You've got drama. It's much more exciting.'

He made her feel wicked and unfaithful, but she still knew she was unsuitable for someone like Steven.

'You can't really want to marry me,' she choked.

'Normally marriage follows an engagement,' he reminded her with a cold look. 'However, I can see now that you're not exactly normal, in spite of my best efforts.'

'I can't marry you, Steven!' She bent her head, tears streaming down her cheeks. 'I couldn't marry you and know you had—had somebody else. Even if it's not Auriel, you're sophisticated and—and so different from me. I could never match you.'

For a minute he just looked at her angrily, and then he reached for her, cupping her unhappy face in warm, strong hands.

'There is nobody else,' he said fiercely. 'There has been nobody else since you were eighteen.'

'It—it's four years.' She was still giving choking little sobs, and he bent and began to kiss her tears away.

'I have enormous reserves of discipline,' he confessed between kisses. 'The only time I lose it is with you. I love you, my crazy girl. I love you and I want you. I've loved you since you were absurdly young. If I had followed my instincts we would have been married as soon as you were legally of age. You were so clearly, wonderfully mine.'

He was speaking now against her lips, murmuring words that dazed her, and slowly the terrible tension and unhappiness began to drain away.

'No more games, darling,' he whispered. 'We've played too many games. The night of the accident—I didn't forget anything. I remembered you said you loved me.'

'But you told me you didn't remember.' She was slowly melting into him, her soft curves fitting into the harder planes of his body, the intense feelings that were always between them taking over her whole mind.

'You were upset, anxious, creeping into my bedroom like a scared little faun, all eyes. I couldn't remind you then. I couldn't let you realise that I knew. You wanted to protect me, my little Georgina, to give yourself to me, and I wanted you so badly, just as I want you now.'

His voice was so soft but there was a burning ardency at the back of it and she felt all sanity going, going, so fast.

'But why did you go off to London straight away?' she asked anxiously. 'I can't help wanting to know, Steven.'

'To get your ring. You said you loved me. I believed you. The fight was over.' He raised his head and looked down at her with heavy eyes, the blue almost drowned by the blackness of pupil. His face was taut with sensuality and her slender arms slowly came up to encircle his neck.

'Steven,' she whispered, her own eyes beginning to feel dazed.

'I sometimes wonder if you do things deliberately,' he said huskily. 'You enrage me as nobody else can, goading me until I can think of nothing else but making love to you. It's always there, isn't it? Waiting to explode between us.'

It was. It had been there for years and she had been trying to bring on this dazzling form of retaliation since she was a teenager, waiting to see the light flare in Steven's eyes. He pulled her close, his hands compelling on her hips, letting her feel the throbbing, hard desire that raged through him.

'With you there are no half-measures,' he said thickly. 'I see you and I want you; nothing else seems to matter except this driving urgency to make you part of me. It's a terrible, wonderful feeling.'

Georgina gave a passionate sob and began to place frenzied little kisses against his face, her hand lying along the silken rasp of his cheek, and he moulded her to his body, holding her tightly, fiercely aroused.

'If you tell me to stop I will,' he groaned.

'No, Steven! Please, don't stop. Please! Please!'

It was all he needed to hear. His hands were shaking as he undressed both of them, and then he swung her into his arms and placed her on the bed, coming to her at once, covering her with kisses.

'I've wanted you for so long,' he whispered. 'I've wanted my bright, wild, beautiful girl lying in my arms until I thought it would send me mad. But you were so young, my darling, not ready at all, and I had to wait.'

'I would have come to you at any time, Steven. I never forgave you for leaving me.'

'I didn't leave you, darling. I went away but you were always there, right in my mind. You were too young, even at eighteen. I had to give you time. I knew you were safe at Kellerdale, safe and loved, but never as I loved you.'

Tears glistened on her lashes and he knew it was no time for talk. He wanted to see her face take on the trance-like look. He wanted to hold her fast as she drifted into ecstasy.

His hands cradled her breasts, coaxing and exciting, and the well-remembered little moans left her lips, making his eyes flare with passion. His lips trailed kisses all over her and she was falling, falling into colour and light, whispering his name.

'Tell me you want me,' he ordered almost harshly, forcing her back to him.

'I want you, Steven.'

'Tell me you love me.

'I love you. I love you.' Her voice was choked, desperate. It was how they were with each other, desire flaring between them of such intensity that it was unbearable.

'Steven!' It was just a small thread of sound, and he pulled her beneath him, parting her thighs.

'It's all right, darling,' he whispered urgently. 'You're mine.'

Nothing could stop her from spinning away. The exquisite pain of his possession brought her momentarily back, her eyes opening to see Steven's face harsh with passion, his blue eyes drowning her, and then she gave a wild little cry, rushing upwards into a new world.

'I'm here, darling. I'm here with you,' Steven said thickly and she knew, everything inside her knew, that this time Steven was there too, lost in her dreamy world, spinning with her like a leaf through the universe. She was part of Steven, her beloved Steven, and when she opened her eyes he would be there.

He was there and she was crying softly, tears streaming down her face as Steven watched her with adoring eyes, making no attempt to stop them. He knew her, understood. Her desperation, her wild desire, was also his own.

'To say I love you would be the understatement of all time,' he said softly. 'There is no word, no expression to tell you how I feel. I think perhaps we knew each other, loved each other long ago in some other time, some other world.'

'Don't say that,' she pleaded gently. 'We might never have found each other.' He smiled at her tenderly, stroking her hot face.

'I would have found you,' he assured her. 'I would have found you if I'd had to search the universe from one lifetime to another.'

His fingers wiped away her tears and she moved languorously, still bewildered by the love that was sweeping over her.

'No,' he ordered softly, his eyes searching each part of her face. 'Forgive me, my love, but I can't let you go yet.'

There was so much tenderness in his voice, in the way he looked at her, that Georgina closed her eyes and wound her arms around his neck, arching against him as he lifted her back into his arms, everything inside her waiting for the fierce, burning passion that flooded over her.

Later they sat in the drawing-room that looked out on to the square. Georgina was wearing one of Steven's bathrobes, the sleeves turned back and the belt tightly tied to keep it on. Even so, it almost reached her toes, and he found it all amusing.

'I feel as if I haven't eaten for weeks,' she said as she tucked into the steak they had both cooked in the kitchen. She had a tray on her knee, her toes curled neatly under her like a small fastidious cat, and Steven leaned back on the settee, watching her, love and amusement shining from his eyes.

When she finally pushed the tray aside she looked down for a minute and then looked directly at him, her honey-gold eyes serious.

'After all that time. Why did you choose to come back when you did?' she asked carefully.

'Ripley.' He said nothing more and she looked quite shocked.

'Jeremy? What had he got to do with it?'

'He was taking you out just a little too often. Mother knew damned well why I went away. She thought it was about time I came back and got my girl.'

'She knew?' Georgina looked at him in amazement and he suddenly laughed.

'I think everyone knew but you,' he mocked. 'I've been frustrated for a very long time. Waiting for you to grow up was something of a trial.'

'I only realised a couple of weeks ago that I'd grown up,' Georgina confessed with a helpless little sigh. 'It was thinking you wanted a mistress, not knowing what to do. I was scared of losing you again and yet I . . .'

'Come and sit here with me,' he ordered when she seemed to be verging on tears. His eyes moved over her with sheer delight as she padded across to him, and then he pulled her into his arms, settling her against his shoulder.

'I have never wanted a mistress,' he assured her gently. 'I want a wife—you. I want you tied to me for good, your head on my pillow, your hand in mine. Didn't I tell you when you were a child I would hold you to that? I didn't know then how true it would be.'

She snuggled against him, her dearest Steven, but she was still scolding softly.

'You let me believe——'

'Shock tactics,' he explained.

'What?'

'Keep still.' He held her closely, caressing her back. 'I've loved you for years, and it was painfully clear that

you were going to battle forever. I knew damned well
you loved me but you were more interested in your fight
than in anything else. I thought once or twice of over-
powering you, but dismissed it as unworthy. I wanted
you so much that it was an agony, so I gave myself a
few weeks to tame you, to bring you to heel.'

'Don't you think it was a bit disgraceful?' She sat up
and looked at him reproachfully, and he grinned into
her aggrieved face.

'Certainly not! If I hadn't been hampered by desire it
would have been most amusing.'

'I suffered!' she reminded him hotly. 'And you made
me work like a slave. *And* you threatened to make me
leave Kellerdale.'

'How very untrue,' he chided. 'You, my wonderful
idiot, will never leave Kellerdale. One day you'll be the
lady of the manor.'

'Oh! I could never manage that,' Georgina said,
looking quite scared.

'You haven't a lot of choice,' he pointed out, pulling
her back to his shoulder. 'Before we leave London we'll
be married.'

'Here?' She shot up again and looked at him with just
a touch of concern.

'Here,' he stated firmly. 'When I came down for your
ring, you may remember, I stayed a while.' He slanted
one dark eyebrow at her and she had the grace to blush
softly. She had thought he was waiting for Auriel, staying
here with her. 'I spent the time arranging a wedding, my
wedding. As far as I could see, the battle had raged quite
long enough. You may be interested to know that you're
getting married two days from now.'

'But...' Her eyes clouded over and he smiled at her
gently.

'But you wanted a pretty wedding? Do you think I
didn't realise that? How does a wedding at a very sweet
little church near here suit you? The wedding lunch at

Claridge's, the honeymoon in the Seychelles. I've ordered the flowers and everything else. You can get your dress tomorrow. We'll collect Rowena when we collect your clothes from her house.'

She smiled up at him, gloriously happy.

'You were very sure of me,' she teased, and he looked down at her, his brilliant blue eyes making her heart leap.

'All my life,' he said softly.

'Steven's girl,' she whispered, and he kissed her with such sweetness that she could hardly breathe.

'What about the family?' she asked as he finally let her go for a minute.

'I'll phone them soon—today. It will give Celia time to rush out and buy yet another expensive outfit, and I'm sure Mother will find something if she searches in the bottom of her wardrobe.'

His amused irony had her laughing. His mother was just about the most elegantly dressed woman she had ever seen.

'I wonder what Malcolm will do now?' she mused after a minute.

'Ah! I might have guessed you'd know,' he murmured against her hair. 'The red-hot phone line, of course.'

'It rather upset Rowena,' she told him quietly, and he jerked her head back, his fingers fastening quite tightly in her hair.

'No plans!' he ordered firmly. 'You and Celia will allow everyone to cope with their own lives; besides,' he said softly, his eyes on her startled lips, 'it will be no use planning, because I'll find out.'

'And how will you manage that, lord and master?' she laughed, looking up at him.

'There is such a place as bed,' he reminded her seductively. 'I'll have every last secret out of you there. And, on that subject, you do realise that you're staying here with me until this wedding?'

'Your mistress, in fact.'

'Just to see what it's like,' he agreed, his eyes smiling into hers. 'Honestly, darling, I can't let you move more than an inch from me. It actually hurts when you're not there.'

'I know.' It hurt not to be close to Steven too. It had always hurt, but now they would be together always, back at Kellerdale, where they belonged. She gave a happy sigh, her mind seeing the wonderful days ahead of them. How right Celia had been with her fortune telling.

'Why didn't you bring Prince with you?' she suddenly asked, beginning to smile. 'You said he wanted to help with the driving.'

Steven gave it a moment of consideration and then shook his head.

'Not on the motorway. That dog has no lane discipline.'

Georgina began to laugh, looking up into the brilliant sapphire eyes. She had him back, completely back, her wonderful, handsome, adored Steven.

'Oh, Steven. I do love you,' she said, smiling into his eyes. 'And you're so funny.'

His face took on that look again, the look that could melt her, and his hand slid into the neck of her robe, caressing her skin.

'I'm funny about you,' he said huskily. 'Come with me again, Georgina, back into that wonderful little world.'

He lifted her and her head came to rest against his shoulder, her lips against his neck. Nobody else could enter their secret world. It was their own place, a place where she had always wanted to be—with Steven.

AN EXCITING NEW SERIAL BY ONE OF THE WORLD'S BESTSELLING WRITERS OF ROMANCE

BARBARY WHARF is an exciting 6 book mini-series set in the glamorous world of international journalism.

Powerful media tycoon Nick Caspian wants to take control of the Sentinel, an old and well established British newspaper group, but opposing him is equally determined Gina Tyrell, whose loyalty to the Sentinel and all it stands for is absolute.

The drama, passion and heartache that passes between Nick and Gina continues throughout the series - and in addition to this, each novel features a separate romance for you to enjoy.

Read all about Hazel and Piet's dramatic love affair in the first part of this exciting new serial.

BESIEGED

Available soon

Price: £2.99

Next month's Romances

Each month, you can choose from a world of variety in romance with Mills & Boon. These are the new titles to look out for next month.

THE GOLDEN MASK ROBYN DONALD

THE PERFECT SOLUTION CATHERINE GEORGE

A DATE WITH DESTINY MIRANDA LEE

THE JILTED BRIDEGROOM CAROLE MORTIMER

SPIRIT OF LOVE EMMA GOLDRICK

LEFT IN TRUST KAY THORPE

UNCHAIN MY HEART STEPHANIE HOWARD

RELUCTANT HOSTAGE MARGARET MAYO

TWO-TIMING LOVE KATE PROCTOR

NATURALLY LOVING CATHERINE SPENCER

THE DEVIL YOU KNOW HELEN BROOKS

WHISPERING VINES ELIZABETH DUKE

DENIAL OF LOVE SHIRLEY KEMP

PASSING STRANGERS MARGARET CALLAGHAN

TAME A PROUD HEART JENETH MURREY

STARSIGN

GEMINI GIRL LIZA GOODMAN